Spies & Stilettos

Also by Liliana Hart

Whiskey, You're The Devil
Whiskey on the Rocks
Whiskey Tango Foxtrot

JJ GRAVES MYSTERIES
Dirty Little Secrets
A Dirty Shame
Dirty Rotten Scoundrel
Down and Dirty
Dirty Deeds

STANDALONE NOVELS/NOVELLAS
All About Eve
Paradise Disguised
Catch Me If You Can
Kill Shot
Breath of Fire

Spies & Stilettos
By Liliana Hart

A MacKenzie Family Novel, Book 18

EVIL EYE
CONCEPTS

Spies & Stilettos
A MacKenzie Family Novel, Book 18
Copyright 2017 Liliana Hart
ISBN: 978-1-942299-86-8

Published by **Evil Eye Concepts, Incorporated**

Acknowledgments

To Liz Berry and MJ Rose. I can't thank you enough for your encouragement, kindness, and patience. Two years ago you took a chance on this idea and ran with it, and I can't imagine anyone doing it better. Thank you.

A huge thanks to Jay Crownover, Lynn Raye Harris, Kaylea Cross, and Gennita Low for each contributing a story in the MacKenzie World. You're some of my favorite authors, and I'm so honored you joined the project.

Jillian Stein, you're amazing. You make my life so much easier, and I want you to know how much you're appreciated. Also, a huge thanks to Kim and the editorial team for all your hard work on this book.

Last but not least, words can't express the gratitude I have for my husband, Scott Silverii. A thank you isn't enough. I'm glad you told me I was going to marry you. I'd do it all over again.

An Introduction to the Mackenzie Family World

Dear Readers,

I'm thrilled to announce the MacKenzie Family World is returning! I asked five of my favorite authors to create their own characters and put them into the world you all know and love. These amazing authors revisited Surrender, Montana, and through their imagination you'll get to meet new characters, while reuniting with some of your favorites.

These stories are hot, hot, hot and packed with action and adventure—exactly what you'd expect from a MacKenzie story. It was pure pleasure for me to read each and every one of them and see my world through someone else's eyes. They definitely did the series justice, and I hope you discover five new authors to put on your auto-buy list.

Make sure you check out Spies and Stilettos, a brand new, full-length MacKenzie novel written by me. This will be the final installment of the MacKenzie series, featuring Brady Scott and Elena Nayal. After eighteen books of my own and ten books written by other bestselling authors in the MacKenzie World, it's going to be difficult to say good-bye to a family I know as well as my own. Thank you for falling in love with the MacKenzies.

So grab a glass of wine, pour a bubble bath, and prepare to Surrender.

Love Always,
Liliana Hart

Available now!

Spies & Stilettos by Liliana Hart
Trouble Maker by Liliana Hart
Rush by Robin Covington
Never Surrender by Kaylea Cross

Avenged by Jay Crownover
Bullet Proof by Avery Flynn
Delta: Rescue by Cristin Harber
Hot Witness by Lynn Raye Harris
Deep Trouble by Kimberly Kincaid
Wicked Hot by Gennita Low
Desire & Ice by Christopher Rice

Chapter One

Elena Nayal knew fear. She knew what it tasted like. What it smelled like. And she knew what it felt like for silent screams to echo relentlessly in the mind.

Her heart pounded and she watched impotently as lives hung in the balance. Her job was to save lives, not to panic, no matter how badly she wanted to. Ink black eyes remained glued to the bank of electronic screens that covered the wall inside the MacKenzie Security HQ Command Center.

"I don't care what it says, Titus." Her voice was calm and commanding, despite the butterflies dancing in her stomach. "I'm telling you to go straight ahead."

"HQ, we're getting overrun out here. I can't afford one wrong turn." Titus was the newest team leader of highly trained operatives that MacKenzie Security had dispatched across the globe. Expanding the operations of MacKenzie Security was an experiment, and it was failing.

Her nails were short and neat, her fingers unadorned, and she typed with quick efficiency as she studied the data and images scrolling across the screens. Her mind was focused, despite the rattled transmissions from Titus. She'd heard his fear. Recognized it. And discarded it. Fear would only get them killed. Her job was to provide the team with an escape route.

She'd never been to Somalia, but she'd spent her nights researching it before the team had left for the mission—it wasn't like she was able to sleep, so she might as well make herself useful.

The mission should've been simple. They were rescuing petroleum researchers from Somali pirates. Those who worked for MacKenzie Security were the best—more than capable enough to get the job done. But what had started as a quick grab-and-go mission had turned into a fight for survival.

"Get us out of here, HQ." Titus's voice broke as he pleaded to a woman he'd never met but now entrusted with his very life.

"I'm working on it," she assured him. "Stay with me, Alpha One. Stay calm. I'll get you out."

Elena was the head of logistics and support for MacKenzie Security. She'd managed high-threat communications over the last several years. It was her responsibility to keep the team leaders informed, aware, and alert to all data relevant to their team's situation. She was their eyes and ears while they were on the ground. Technology was a beautiful thing. Especially the kind of technology MacKenzie Security had access to.

Although she was over nine thousand miles away from the city of Merca, she was completely plugged in to Titus and the nine other warriors running blind through the East African jungle.

"Alpha One, maintain your course," she said. "I'm programming new coordinates into your navigator that will allow you to meet the next chopper evac from a less hostile position."

"Screw that. Send in backup." Titus was letting emotion control him, and she could sense his unraveling. "We need more guns on the ground, HQ."

She shook her head, even though she knew he couldn't see her. The team was on their own. You never risked more men to rescue the rescuers.

"Alpha One," she said. "Are you there?"

"Go, HQ."

"You're it. There's no backup."

Her eyes scanned the geographic navigation maps, and a live-feed satellite image of the ten men—each living, breathing soul nothing more than a blur of red on the screen. And she was responsible for getting them the hell out of there.

A powerful insurgent group called al Shahaab was creating chaos for the African governments of Kenya and Somalia to capitalize on the abundant wealth that lay below the surface—black gold. Global petroleum developmental companies couldn't move in because of the extreme violence. But like in all things, money was a great motivator.

BrexCorp, a United Kingdom-based petroleum firm, had hired MacKenzie Security to protect their staff. Their CEO had relied on the security firm in the past and shared a close friendship with Declan MacKenzie, the head of MacKenzie Security, though all the MacKenzies had a stake in the company. But the Somali pirates had far outnumbered the staff and agents assigned to them and they'd been taken for ransom.

There was a lot more riding on the line than just the safety of the BrexCorp staff, though that was the priority. MacKenzie Security's reputation was on the line, along with Declan's.

"Damn it, HQ," Titus said. "You've led us to a dead end. Kiss our asses good-bye because this fight won't last long." He ripped into her and she felt every lash of his tongue, though she knew it was desperation, not hate, that coated his words.

"Turn left," she told him.

"Repeat. Taking gunfire. Repeat, command."

"Turn left, Alpha One."

She kept her voice steady and calm. He needed her to be his rock, even though her heart was pounding and fear clutched her belly. It was now her job to get them into a safe location to allow him to regain a cool head and revert to his training.

"You want us to turn left?" he asked, and then he laughed. "Fuck that. Straight ahead is a cliff and left is a giant rock wall. Right looks like the better option. Sorry, HQ, but your eyesight is warped. Thanks for nothing."

Elena stood and felt the slow burn of anger beneath her skin. Reckless bastard. He was going to get them all killed. She studied the large bank of touchscreens on the wall, and her finger traced across the detailed images of where Alpha Team was stranded. What was she missing?

She pressed three fingers against the screen and zoomed in. Greens and blues with jagged lines of red came into focus, outlining the areas that surrounded them.

"HQ to Alpha One, if you proceed to the right, you will die. If you disobey my instructions, you'll be acting on your own. Our contract with you is very clear about your duty to follow directions. This isn't a standard military op. If you manage to stay alive, I can assure you it'll be the last mission you're assigned to."

"We're taking bullets," Titus screamed. "I don't care what the contract says. Get us out of this shit."

Elena blocked out his comments. Time was running out. It was time she took the reins from Alpha One. He clearly didn't have what it took to command, and now that command would fall to her. She just hoped like hell she could get through to them before lives were lost.

"This is HQ to Alpha Team," she snapped. "If you want to live, disregard Alpha One's orders. He's been relieved of command. You'll see a sheer rock wall to your left. There's a slight gap that leads into a basin at the ten o'clock position. Set up on the west side of that wall, inside the basin, and use the narrow gap to eliminate the enemy."

"Roger that, HQ. Moving left." It was a female voice that

answered, and Elena checked her roster to the corresponding red blur of a body on the screen. *Megan Murchison.* Thank God someone had some common sense.

Elena blew out a huge breath of relief and dropped back into the chair, turning off her comms for a second so she could take a breath in peace, but the danger wasn't over yet. All she could do was watch as nine fuzzy, reddish silhouettes followed her directions and moved left. All but one. Alpha One stood alone.

"Idiot," she whispered.

Elena checked the settings on her screen option to make sure there were image and audio recordings of the mission. She'd been through administrative panel reviews many times and knew the drill, and she'd be damned if she went down because some hot-shot rookie commander with more balls than brains decided it was a good day to die.

The truth of the matter was, the business of security on a global scale was dangerous. Agents didn't always come back alive. But someone had to be accountable. Because of her position behind the control panel, that person was usually her. She'd held up under briefings when agents were killed in the line of duty. Her record stood for itself, and she had the documentation to back it up.

She'd always been able to withstand the pressure. The job was her life. It consumed her. Only something with that much intensity could make her forget the nightmares that left her sweating and screaming. She had a feeling documentation was about to become critical for her own survival within MacKenzie Security. Titus was signing his own death warrant, and she wanted no part of it.

Dread knotted her gut. "Move, you fool," she said, but he couldn't hear her because she'd turned her comms off. She swiftly turned them back on and said, "Alpha One, move in with the others."

But his red pixelated form began to move along the steep cliff's edge in the opposite direction.

"Dammit, listen to me. Retreat to safety." She zoomed in on a growing horde of what she knew to be indigenous rebels encroaching on the dead-end intersection where her men were trapped.

Nausea roiled in her stomach as she watched the large amoeba-like collection of red silhouettes on the satellite screen overtake Titus. He was no longer distinguishable among them, the blurs of red forming into a larger image

"No, no, no," she said, shaking her head in disbelief as Titus's vitals flatlined on her screen. She'd never known him, but she would grieve for his loss. Just like she always did.

Elena composed herself. She was an expert at pushing down her emotions to the point that no one knew she was screaming inside. This time would be no different. Notifications would have to be made to Declan, but her report would be just that. A report accompanied by the recording of the event.

The door to the communication room opened, and her head snapped around to see who the intruder was. She didn't have time for distractions, and she almost growled an order to get out before she saw Brady Scott's quick grin of greeting. She didn't return the smile. Talk about distractions.

It was hard for her to deal with Brady on a good day. The Navy SEAL commander was two hundred pounds of solid muscle packed into a six-foot-two frame. His jaw was square, his lips full, and his eyes an unusual shade of green with tiny gold flecks around the pupil. He was the nicest man she'd ever met, and even when she'd made it clear she had no desire to be his friend, he'd been friendly to her anyway. He'd also been on the team Declan had sent to rescue her after a group of Alexander Ramos's men had beaten and repeatedly raped her, leaving her broken and nearly dead on a dirt street in Mexico.

She always wondered if that was the image Brady saw when he looked at her. Naked and bruised and bleeding, begging for them to let her die because the pain was so great when they'd tried to move her.

Her body had healed. And she'd learned to live with her past. Or at least bury it enough to function. But Brady had kept showing up, smiling at her despite her rudeness to him, and subtly making it known that he wasn't at all deterred by her attitude.

"They make it out yet?" he asked.

She shook her head no and tapped the earpiece of her headset so he'd know the mission wasn't complete. She muted her comms again.

He nodded and came into the room, closing the door behind him. "I thought mission ops had them in and out with civilians in tow in less than an hour, tops?"

He leaned toward the primary display board and squinted at the topographical map.

"Wow, coming into this command center always gives me technology envy. We've got nothing like this for the SEALs," Brady murmured. "They always save the good stuff for the private sector."

Much like she'd done before, he used his fingers to swipe at the wall screen, homing in on the ground team and the unfolding chaos halfway across the world. They'd taken cover in the rock crevice and had been able to use it as a shield and a way to slowly pick off their attackers as they tried to reach them. All she could do was sit by helplessly and listen to the sound of shouts and gunfire, watching the vitals screen to see if there would be any more deaths on her watch.

She couldn't tell what Brady was thinking as he watched it all unfold. He blinked a few times, almost as if he wasn't quite sure what he was seeing, and then he jabbed the screen for a quick zoom.

"What the fuck is happening?" he demanded.

Elena's shoulders stiffened and heat flooded her cheeks. His outburst caught her off guard. She'd seen him bark out orders, and she'd seen him struggle to hold on to his temper. But he'd never lost that control around her. He was always so…careful. Like what had happened to her seven years ago had made her too fragile to be real with. Everyone treated her like that. And she hated it.

She was tired of being treated as if she was going to break at any moment. No one knew how strong she really was. How much determination she'd managed to forge just to live from one day to the next. She remembered exactly how many bones had broken in her body—seven—and the excruciating pain of having her shoulder torn out of socket. And the searing smell of burnt flesh as they branded her thigh while another man crawled between her legs and grunted and sweated on top of her until he found his release.

After that, nothing could break her again. The MacKenzies had saved her. They'd made sure she'd gotten the medical care she'd needed, and then they'd given her a purpose by giving her a job. Her days and nights were all the same. She trained—because she'd determined she'd never be helpless again. Never again would she be taken without a fight. She worked—because it occupied her mind. And when her body and mind were too tired to function, she collapsed into an exhausted sleep, only to be bombarded with the nightmares of her past and woken with the feel of hands around her throat and the smells of everything that had happened in that filthy alleyway.

No one had ever questioned her work. She was too good at it. She put too much time and research into everything she did. But to have Brady question her set her temper off.

"What the hell does it look like?" she replied. "The mission went belly up, and now I'm trying to coordinate who's going to rescue the rescue team."

He looked at her in surprise and held up a hand as a peace offering. "Hey, I'm sorry," he said. "It was supposed to be an in-and-out op. I'm the one who recommended the new TL. I wanted his first mission to be a success. He's got a lot of promise."

"He's gone," she told him gently.

"What?" he asked, the disbelief evident in his voice. Then he said again, "What? How is that even possible? What the hell happened out there?"

She couldn't deal with him right now. She'd never seen him that upset, and she realized she'd come to rely on his constancy over the years.

"Let me do my job," she told him. "This isn't over yet, and I'll give everyone a briefing once it's played out."

"Shit, Elena, what's left to play out? We sent a ten-man team to rescue a group of BrexCorp hostages, and the only thing I see on the screen is the enemy taking over. Your job is to be their eyes and ears when they can't. To keep them safe. They're putting their lives on the line and they're relying on you."

Her brows lifted and her hands balled in to fists at her side. "What's left?" she asked incredulously. "You want to know what's left to play out?"

She stepped from behind the console and wedged herself between him and the wall screens. She was too pissed to notice how close she'd gotten. She made it a point to always stand at least an arm's length from anyone. She didn't like to be touched.

Her fingers moved fast and furious across the screen, pulling up the image she wanted. And then she slapped her hand against it to drive home her point.

"They're what's left," she said, her chest heaving. "These are the nine men who almost died in the line of duty because their team leader refused to follow my orders."

"Instructions," Brady corrected coolly.

"Fine, instructions," she said. "The fact remains that they're still there, and they still need me. You don't have to tell me what my job is. I just listened to a man die. I know what the hell my job is better than anyone."

His nostrils flared as he tried to get control of his temper, and he took a couple of calming breaths.

"What's their progress?" he pressed.

This wasn't the Brady Scott she knew asking the question. This was Brady Scott, the SEAL commander. The seasoned veteran who'd seen and done more than most people could hope to in a lifetime.

She rolled her shoulders back and reined in her temper. She was going to have a hell of a workout later. That's where she got out most of her anger. She never let the others see when she was affected by something, and she didn't know why she was acting so out of character now. Maybe because Brady was acting different.

"I don't know because I've been fending off your attacks since you entered my workspace. Let me do my job," she repeated.

Brady nodded and tried to smile, but the tension was etched on his face.

The MacKenzies had made her feel safe since her rescue seven years before. They'd given her a home. And a family of sorts, though she'd never accepted the invitations to gatherings they'd invited her to. Her father was dead, killed by the same cartel that had destroyed her, and her blood family was scattered and few and far between.

Someone like Brady Scott would never truly know what it meant to be alone. He was as much a MacKenzie as those that had MacKenzie blood. His brother Brant was married to Darcy MacKenzie, and his sister Bayleigh was married to Cade MacKenzie. So Brady felt comfortable enough coming and going from the MacKenzie compound, just like he'd feel comfortable questioning her ability.

She'd never be able to repay the MacKenzies for their generosity. But she wouldn't take the blame for something that wasn't her fault. She'd spent years trying to understand that what the cartel had done to her wasn't deserved. She'd been the one to turn over information about the cartel to the MacKenzies, and the guilt ate at her. Her father was dead because of that information. It had been hard for her twenty-year-old mind to understand that her rape was not punishment for his death.

She realized how close she was standing to Brady, and she quickly put distance between them, making her way back behind the console. He was too big. Too overpowering. And there was something about him that frightened her on a level she didn't understand. She'd been dead inside since the cartel had taken her innocence, but it was hard to remember she was dead inside when he was around. There were sparks of something—she just wasn't sure how to categorize it.

She chewed on her top lip and debated whether or not to apologize. Titus's death had shaken her. He'd been so defiant, and he'd paid the ultimate price. And there was part of her that wondered if she could've done more to save him, could've handled it a different way.

"Look," he said with a sigh. "I don't mean to be a jerk. I just wasn't expecting any of this when I came in. I thought the mission would be marked as a success, and I was going to try to persuade you to go to lunch with me."

"You know I always say no," she told him.

"You'll change your mind one day if I keep asking," he said with a confidence that made her want to shake her head. "But truly, I'm sorry. Focus on getting those guys out of there. They're what's important right now."

Elena exhaled in relief and felt things shift back to normal between them. As normal as they could be. She never let anyone get too close, but Brady had wormed his way into her life, so he was a common fixture, as if he was supposed to be there. Though she'd often go months without seeing him if he was on assignment. But he always took the time to find her—a soft word or a funny joke—an invitation to lunch or dinner that she never took him up on. He was always just…there. And more often than not, he was there when she needed him most. There to hold the punching bag when she needed to let out her anger. And there to lift her spirits when she'd relived her torture during the night. She'd come to rely on him in ways she hadn't realized, and their current exchange had shaken her.

Only a couple of minutes had passed since he'd entered her domain, but it felt like too much had happened in such a short amount of time. She focused back on the screen, back on the agents on the ground who needed her.

"If anyone can do it, you can," Brady said, opening the door to leave. "I'll see you at the briefing."

She nodded and felt something catch in her throat. Just a small word of encouragement and she felt like blubbering like a baby. She was losing her mind.

The door eased shut and the room returned to a dim, cool chamber of electronic activity. She knew the confrontation had cost her valuable, life-saving moments. She tuned back in to the radio network controls so she could hear transmissions from the other team members.

"HQ to Alpha Team," she dispatched. "Status report."

Silence…

She'd seen them there only moments before—nine red blurs hiding in the rock crevice. It was possible the thickness of the rock wall was limiting their radio coverage.

"HQ to Alpha Team, respond."

"Alpha Two," a familiar voice said, though the words were broken by static. It was Murchison.

"Status, Alpha Two?"

Nerves danced in her stomach as more static came over the comms. She reached for the bottle of water to wet her dry throat.

More static came over the line, followed by Murchison's voice again. "Narrow," she said.

"The basin opening?" Elena asked for clarification.

"Very narrow," Murchison repeated.

"Shit. Can you breach through?"

"Please," Murchison begged. "Send help. We need help."

Elena felt the bottom drop out of her stomach as the line to all comms went dead. Her link to Alpha Team was gone, and they were all alone. She'd sent them to their deaths.

"Oh, my God," she whispered. "What have I done?"

Chapter Two

Declan MacKenzie paced the spacious conference room like a caged tiger. He caught his reflection in the large mirror at the end of the room and his gray eyes shimmered silver with anger. The scar that ran across his jawline was stark white. No one would know he was angry unless they knew him well. He was relaxed beneath the expensive suit he wore, though his skin vibrated with the heat of his rage.

He hated suits. But when he'd left field ops and started MacKenzie Security, he'd understood the need for his image to change. People didn't feel comfortable investing millions of dollars in a company where the president wore BDUs and a thigh holster, even though that's certainly how *he* was most comfortable.

He stopped pacing and ran his hand over his closely shorn hair. The carpet was thick and a deep gray. And pale gray walls were stark with the exception of two paintings that had been used for payment on a particularly difficult mission.

He'd spent a day in meetings, and his head was pounding. All he wanted was to go home, forget about the day, and bury himself deep inside his wife. He'd had to leave early that morning to make his first meeting, and he'd been surprised as hell when he'd gotten a text during that meeting of his wife wearing nothing but a pout on her face. She hadn't liked that he'd left without waking her up properly. To say the rest of that meeting had been spent uncomfortably would've been an understatement.

Sophia had been making noises recently about having another baby, and he was more than happy to accommodate her, but he was worried she was putting too much strain on her body and her time since they already had a two- and a three-year-old running around the house.

He'd never known he was capable of the kind of love he had for his wife and children. Sophia was the light to his darkness, and he'd never have really lived without her. And he found that the more he loved her, the more his priorities had shifted. He had a duty to his country to keep it safe. But his first duty was to his family, and he'd do whatever it took to keep Sophia happy. And if that meant keeping her pregnant for the next ten years, then that's what he'd do. The core of the MacKenzies had always been family.

He'd been on his way home to make things up to his wife when he'd gotten the alert from Elena about the loss of Titus Dean. Things had gone downhill from there once he'd started receiving the reports.

Now he was stuck in a conference room waiting on his agents to show up and tell him about the clusterfuck that was the Somalia mission instead of making love to his wife.

His brother Shane was the first to arrive. Shane had been a Navy SEAL commander before he'd lost his leg in an explosion a couple of years before. It hadn't been an easy road to recovery, and Declan had to give a lot of the credit to Shane's wife, Lacey, just for her pure determination and unwillingness to let him give up.

There was no doubt when you looked at any of the MacKenzies that they were related. They all shared the dark hair of their father, and the boys were all about the same size, though

Cade was a couple inches taller than the rest of them.

Shane was a different man than he'd been two years before. Declan had spent many nights wondering if they'd lose him after the loss of his leg had taken away the career he'd loved more than anything. But he'd battled back, and MacKenzie R&D had given Shane the opportunity to try a prosthetic prototype.

As Shane walked down the long hallway toward the conference room, it was impossible to tell he was missing a limb. His stride was as cocky as ever, and there was no limp. His mouth was quirked to one side like it was when he had something amusing to share.

"Whew, you look pissed as hell," Shane said, clapping him on the shoulder and entering the conference room.

"And I thought I was hiding it so well," Declan answered. "What has you in such a good mood?"

Shane's mouth twitched again. "It's my day off. Or it *was* my day off until you called me in. I went fishing with Dad this morning, and then had a long lunch with Lacey."

By the relaxed posture and stupid grin on his face, Declan was guessing they did more than have lunch.

"How's Dad?" he asked.

The last year had been hard for all of them after losing their mother to enemy hands. But there had been a time after her death when they thought they might lose their dad too.

He and their mother had truly been one, and when she'd been killed part of him had died right along with her. They'd barely gotten her buried when their robust, larger-than-life father had a heart attack. He'd survived, but his spirit wasn't the same, and Declan couldn't blame him. He didn't know what he'd do if anything ever happened to Sophia.

"He seemed okay," Shane said. "He likes to keep up to date on the parts of the business we can talk about." James MacKenzie had been a career Marine, and since his retirement he'd turned to running the MacKenzie ranch full time, with the help of various family members. "He just needs to keep busy. Though he said he barely has a moment's peace all day. Someone is always stopping by the house to make sure he's taken care of. He said he never realized how many damned grandkids he had and that we should learn to keep it in our pants."

That made Declan grin, because it sounded exactly like their father to say something like that. "Which is why he's got five kids himself."

"That's what I told him," Shane said, smiling. "And then he laughed and told me that MacKenzies weren't meant for celibacy from their wives. He said in another hundred years we'd probably have populated the whole state of Montana."

"I wouldn't be surprised," Declan said. "Sophia wants another baby."

"And I'm sure you're so against giving her one," Shane scoffed.

"Not at all," Declan said. "I'm more than happy to do my part to populate the state."

"Well, you'd better get busy. You know it's more fun when all the cousins are the same age. Lacey and I were going to announce at dinner tonight. She's about three months along."

Declan broke out into a smile, his earlier anger and frustration forgotten for just a moment. He couldn't have been more ecstatic for his brother. After everything Shane had been through, he deserved to live the rest of his life in happiness.

Declan reached over and wrapped Shane in a hug, slapping him on the back a couple of times. "Hey, congratulations, man. It's going to change your life forever. In the best possible way."

"Lacey has been sick as a dog," Shane said. "It's hard to watch."

"Wait until childbirth. It doesn't get any easier to see the woman you love in pain. But she'll mostly forgive you for the whole ordeal after the baby is born."

At that moment, Audrey Sharpe-Ryan came in and raised a brow at the two of them. "Am I interrupting?" she asked. "I thought we were having a meeting. You two look like you're about to break out into song. This is very awkward."

Declan could look at Audrey objectively and state with a hundred percent honesty that she was one of the most beautiful women he'd ever seen. She was tall in stature and she carried herself with the kind of quiet dignity that some were born with. Her face was flawless, her cheekbones high, and her lips full. Her eyes were black as night and fringed with thick lashes and brows. Her thick black hair was pulled into a high ponytail, and she wore black BDUs and a gray tank top with the MacKenzie Security logo over the breast.

The tank top revealed the scar of an old gunshot wound at her shoulder. She had two more to match on her chest that weren't visible, and scars all across her back and stomach. She'd had a hell of a career and lived to tell about it.

She was a former Mossad agent who'd been captured and tortured while on a mission. Declan had been the CIA agent to free her and bring her back to the United States for sanctuary. Her cover had been blown as Mossad, but her skills were invaluable and she'd been absorbed into covert ops for a different country. Declan had recruited her after he'd started MacKenzie Security because she was, quite simply, one of the best agents he'd ever seen. It was a bonus that she'd fallen in love with and married Archer Ryan, who'd been one of his agents since the beginning of the company.

"You're a riot," Shane said. "I thought you guys were OOC. When did you get back?"

"This morning," she said, taking one of the seats on the opposite side of the table so she was facing the door. "Archer caught some kind of twenty-four-hour virus on the way back and he's sleeping it off at the house. I was tempted to ignore the summons to come and stay home with him. Those long flights kick my ass every time. I haven't been to bed yet."

Elena came into the room with her laptop and a thick file, and Declan's brows rose when he saw Brady come in behind her. He hadn't been invited to the meeting since he technically wasn't an employee of MacKenzie Security. But the SEAL team he commanded—Shane's former team—often accompanied them on missions if they were on leave.

Shane and Brady were best friends, and they gave a quick knuckle bump before Brady took a seat at the far end of the conference table near Elena. Declan had been watching Brady dance around Elena for seven years. It had been almost painful at times. They all remembered what she'd looked like that day they found her in the alley. It wasn't a picture that could ever be erased from their minds, no matter how hard they tried.

Brady remembered that night as well as he did, and there'd been something in him that had raged when he'd seen the broken slip of a girl left in the street to die. It had been Brady who'd exacted her revenge in the most brutal of ways. He'd hunted her attackers down like dogs and given them no mercy. They hadn't been hard to find. They'd been drunk and bragging about it in a little cantina.

Declan had never been sure Elena had truly healed, and he often wondered if he'd made the right decision in all but forcing her to belong with them. They'd wanted to save her and protect her, especially after she'd showed such bravery in leading them to taking down Alexander Ramos and disbanding his cartel. But she'd always kept her distance. There had always been that little speck of fear in her eyes, even after her body had healed and she'd hardened herself to all emotions.

Brady had watched her and waited, slowly extending a hand, like one would do with a skittish animal, until she got used to him being there. But there was something inside Elena that was broken, and no amount of extending a hand had been accepted by her, though Brady had gotten closer than anyone.

"I sent you all the transmissions through email," Elena said, "but I brought you a hard copy as well."

Declan felt his anger return and had to work to tamp it down until he heard all the facts. He had no idea how what should've been a straightforward mission could've gone to hell so quickly.

"Brady," Declan said, arching a brow. "I didn't realize you'd be joining us."

Brady grinned unapologetically. "You never know when I might come in handy." He tilted his head toward Elena, and he couldn't have made it more clear that he was there for her and her alone. Declan could understand and respect that kind of loyalty.

"Now that we're all here," he said, "let's figure out why the hell we lost an agent out there, and why nine more are missing."

"Holy shit," Shane said, sitting up in his chair. "Is this the Somalia mission? I thought that was a quick in and out?"

"Nothing is ever that simple when human nature is involved," Elena said, her voice cool and even.

Declan dimmed the lights and clicked the remote he'd left on the table. An image of a red-headed, green-eyed man appeared on the wall.

"Titus Dean," Declan said. "I'm going to have to explain to his wife of six months why her husband is never coming home again."

He saw the grief in Elena's eyes as she studied the photo. She'd never seen Titus or any of the Alpha Team before. Putting faces to the blurry red images on the computer screen didn't help her stay cool and dispassionate when the shit started to hit the fan. But now she was seeing that loss of life up close and personal. Declan *wanted* her to see Titus up close and personal. Because he wanted her to remember, next time she was on the boards, that there were real people at the other end. Maybe next time she'd take a little more caution before sending them into a trap.

"He was a twenty-six-year-old former Airborne Ranger. This was his first mission as team leader. And his last. The mission was simple. He and Alpha Team were assigned to evacuate a civilian offshore oil exploration research team for BrexCorp."

Elena sat stoically in her chair, her back straight and her fingers laced in front of her. She knew the gravity of their position. A mistake of this magnitude could bring down everything his entire family had sacrificed for.

Shane whistled as he read the intel from the screen. "Somalia is never to be underestimated," he said. "Right, Brady? We had a couple of close calls on more than one occasion."

"It's a damned viper's nest," Brady said. "They're their own worst enemy. I'm guessing the locals didn't take kindly to good old capitalism."

"You'd be right," Declan said. "Rebels began charging the mostly unguarded compound once they saw the helicopters. Not sure what triggered the all-out assault on the complex, but I guess the choppers spooked them. Titus and his team shoved the last civies on a chopper and fled on foot to keep from becoming victims."

Audrey sighed. "And there's mistake number one. Why the hell would they run into the jungle?"

"Where else were they supposed to go?" Elena's voice was sharp, and Declan knew she'd taken the criticism as a personal attack.

"Because it's like running from a shark and jumping into the ocean," Audrey said.

"There was nowhere else to run," Elena argued.

Audrey leaned onto the table. "That's the point. Why did they run?"

"Because they were being attacked," Elena said, but her

cheeks were flushed and Declan knew she recognized Audrey's point.

"These men are warriors, fighting local insurgents with little to no training. They're not track stars. Which option do you think they'll be more successful at?"

"Audrey," Brady said. "That's harsh."

"No," Elena said. "She's right. I see it now." She looked at Declan. "I apologize. I didn't see them standing to fight as an option. Training has always taught me to avoid engagement unless necessary."

"Which is why I'm keeping an open mind at the moment," he said. "Experience and instinct trumps training, and the situation the team was in today was more complicated than any of us thought."

"You can't think that I'd purposefully lead them into harm's way," Elena said. "None of my training or past experiences allowed for what would happen when the team leader refused to follow orders."

"Instructions," Shane interjected.

Elena's head snapped toward Shane. "Sorry, instructions." But she didn't sound sorry, and Declan raised his brows. He'd never seen Elena lose her cool. She'd been like a robot for seven years, and he was almost relieved to see a crack in her armor. Despite the span of time, she'd never fully healed, and he'd almost lost hope that she would.

"There's a difference," Shane said, shrugging, though Declan could tell he was surprised by her attitude as well. "A huge difference."

"You think I don't know there's a difference?" Elena said, standing. "I've given instructions for exactly three hundred and thirty-seven different and successful operations since I began managing logistics and support years ago. I know the difference between instructions and orders. I know my place here. And it's okay, because I owe so much to your family, Declan. But the fact of the matter is that Titus put himself and his team in danger because of his own foolish choices. Now we just have to figure out if the next move is to plan for a rescue or a recovery. It's all in the transcripts."

"You're entitled to your opinion," Declan said. "And I'll review the transcripts. But I've still got nine men unaccounted for."

Declan turned off the image on the wall and tossed the remote back onto the table. He paced the length of the room a couple of times, trying to think through all the scenarios. Everyone knew him well enough to not interrupt. He was tired. And when it came down to it, he cared more about the men on the ground and the potential loss of lives than he did about losing their reputation or future contracts.

He dropped into the chair at the head of the table and tilted his head toward Elena. "Has it really been three hundred and thirty-seven missions?"

"Exactly that many," she said stiffly.

"You're a hell of an asset to us, Elena," he said. "We'll get this figured out. I know you did what you could to get them out of there."

"It's my duty," she said. "It's what I'm expected to do."

Declan saw Brady flinch out of the corner of his eye. The boy was a goner. And Declan had a feeling he was going to get his heart smashed to bits before it was over.

"You've never been just a duty to us," he told her. "I hope you know that."

* * * *

Elena walked the half mile from the main offices to the building where her command center was located. She needed to clear her head and let the July sun beat down on her shoulders. The walled compound nestled deep in the foothills of Surrender, Montana, and she loved seeing the mountains behind them and the clear blue of the lake that sat on the property. She'd never gotten used to the long, snowy winters, but she loved this time of year.

The MacKenzie Security's operations base was in a remote location to ensure anonymity and safety for all who worked or trained on site. It was a gorgeous section of their sprawling ranch. It had been a good place for Elena, but now she was wondering if it was still the best place for her.

She'd been here for seven years. She'd worked three hundred and thirty-seven missions in the command center. But she didn't feel like she really belonged anywhere. Maybe it was time to move on. They'd all been so kind to her that leaving would be difficult—unless they didn't care if she left. It was hard to tell after the meeting in the conference room.

She'd collected all of the audio and video transmissions from the Somalia situation and secured it in an encrypted folder she shared with Declan. She'd titled it *Merca / Titus Rescue*. Her assistant, Willa, continued to monitor video feeds and satellite transmissions from the region. She'd even tapped into the state military and local militias for reports or gossip of security forces being killed or captured. It was radio silent. She had no idea where her nine remaining men were, even though there hadn't been any changes to their vital signs. They were still alive. They were just lost. And it was eating her up inside.

She knew what it felt like to be trapped and hurt, and to think that no one would ever come for you, no matter how much you begged for help. She couldn't imagine leaving anyone else in that same position. But she had.

The reinforced steel building that housed the command center sat off by itself, and when she used her badge to open the door, a cold blast of air chilled her skin.

"Elena," Willa said, turning from her computer station to face her. "You had a message alert pop up on Cryptocat. Otherwise, it's been quiet. You okay? You're looking kind of pale."

"I'm fine, thanks. Just low on sleep. I'll take over if you want to catch a break."

"I'm not going to turn that down," Willa said, grinning. "Did you see all of those SEALs that Brady brought to the complex? Yum, yum. It's like Christmas around here whenever the SEALs go on leave and decide to spend it in Surrender."

"Be careful," Elena said, raising a brow. "Those are the kind of men where it's easy to bite off more than you can chew."

"Sugar, I hope so," Willa said, winking. "I have no intention of settling down any time soon. I've got work I love, my son, and a stable life for him thanks to Declan and my Uncle Archer. I plan on taking advantage of the perks. God wouldn't put men like that on this planet if he didn't want a woman to appreciate the creation."

Elena wasn't a hundred percent sure how to answer that. She spent most of her time avoiding looking at men.

"Just be careful," Elena called out again as the door closed behind Willa, leaving her alone.

She scrolled through the computer network's screen before locating the red marker in her encrypted messaging service. She used Cryptocat as a way of communicating with the MacKenzies, but seldom anytime other than that. She typed in her password, and then waited to be connected.

The door beeped as someone scanned their badge at the door, and Elena figured Willa must have forgotten something. The door swung open and she was surprised to see Brady there.

"Hey," he said. "Am I interrupting?"

"No," she said. "Of course not." And then she saw Declan step in behind him and she froze. She hadn't had enough time to work off her anger and disappointment from their meeting. She needed some space before she could make any decisions about her future. But she owed Declan her life, and she'd never forget it.

"I'm sorry I lost my temper during the briefing," she told him. "It won't happen again."

"Actually," he said, "it doesn't change the circumstances, but it was nice to see. I wanted to tell you that Shane and I are leaving for South Africa. We'll be connecting with one of our foreign security teams currently working in the Middle East. Those contractors will connect with us in Mogadishu. We'll send an advance team into the region south of the port of bananas just in case we get a lead on where my men are."

"Port of bananas?" Elena asked. She was familiar with the region but she'd never heard of that one before.

"That's what they call the big shipping region at the Port of Merca," Brady interjected, cracking a smile.

Declan's face was humorless. "I need you to coordinate a secure location for us to bunk and establish an operations command center."

"I can do that." Elena scribbled notes on her day planner. "Anything else?"

"Not unless you want to go explain to my wife why I'm having to leave the country for an unknown amount of time to fix this mess." He saluted his good-bye and shut the door behind him.

Elena couldn't hold back the tears, and she quickly turned away from Brady so he didn't see them.

"Elena," he said, coming up behind her.

She could feel his presence, but he didn't touch her. No one ever touched her. And then he did the unexpected. His hands lightly caressed her arms. She shuddered and panic wanted to fill her, but she took a breath and stared at his reflection in the computer screen. If she saw his face, she wouldn't think of the other faceless men who'd left bruises where Brady now stroked. She slowly started to relax, and she let the heat of his hands seep into her.

"You can't let him get to you," Brady said. "He's taking this hard. I've known Dec a long time, and he feels responsible for every life under his command."

"Of course," she said. The guilt was eating her up. "He has every right to feel that way. I screwed up. I understand."

"I don't think you do," he said.

She moved out of his hold and was able to breathe steadily again. It had been a hell of a day, and she was hanging on by a thread. She needed a good workout, something that would leave her so exhausted she wouldn't be able to help but sleep. But first she had to get rid of Brady.

"I've got work to do," she told him. "I'm not on leave like you are."

He flinched as if she'd struck him, but he covered it with a smile that didn't quite reach his eyes.

"Sure," he said. "Catch you later."

She collapsed as soon as he closed the door behind him. How could she be upset with them after all they'd done to get her back on both feet? But she *was* upset. She was angry. And she was hurt that Declan hadn't given her the benefit of the doubt. She'd done what she thought was right. But it hadn't been good enough.

All good things come to an end.

With her decision made, Elena jotted detailed notes for Willa to follow in securing Declan's instructions for their mission in Somalia. It was time for Willa to be given more responsibility if the MacKenzies used her as a replacement once Elena left.

She guzzled a bottle of room temperature water and allowed the emotion from the day to slip from her shoulders. Maybe she'd skip the workout and go straight for the wine. It wasn't like anyone would know. Her tiny cabin was secluded back in the trees, away from the others. Maybe if she had enough wine, she'd just pass out and sleep a whole night through. Though it hadn't worked the time she'd tried it before. In fact, it had made the nightmares worse.

She scrolled through the communications scanner channel just in case there was any news about the missing men. Not a word. She moused over her Cryptocat app and saw the message notification.

"So much for trust," she said. She'd assured Declan that he'd be notified once their meeting location was secured in Mogadishu. There was no reason for him to send her another reminder.

Elena accepted what had been taken from her by those savages seven years before, but try as she might, it was impossible to harden her heart completely. She felt the responsibility of those lives weighing on her shoulders.

She clicked on the secure message, wondering what else Declan might have to throw at her. But it wasn't Declan's words that filled the screen.

Time to come home, puta.

The bile rose in her throat and she hunched over the console, gagging as she realized what the message meant. They weren't all dead, as she'd been told. They'd come back for her.

Chapter Three

Brady looked up at the vast Montana sky and breathed deep. The stars were bright, giving off plenty of light. He was a Texas boy by birth, but he loved it here. Even the winters.

He sat on his porch, a beer in hand, and wondered what the hell was wrong with him that he was in love with a woman who didn't want to be loved. He'd barely had the thought when he saw the woman in question moving through the dark like a thief, a duffel bag slung over her shoulder.

"Elena, where are you going?" Brady called after her.

"I've had enough," she said, picking up her pace.

"What do you mean you've had enough? Who will watch the board?"

"Fuck the board," she said. "If you care so much about the board, then you watch it."

"What the hell?" he said, confused. He sprinted up ahead of her along the paved pathway that ran throughout the complex. Chirps of crickets and the occasional flare from lightning bugs added a charming background to an otherwise tense encounter.

"What is going on, Elena?"

She stopped short of running into him, but didn't answer.

He gently touched her shoulder and then dropped his hand to

his side when she flinched. There were tears in her eyes, and for a brief moment he saw the terrified young woman he'd rescued seven years before. Something was horribly wrong.

"I don't know who did it, but I won't stay here," she said. "Someone would have to hate me to do something like that. It had to be someone with the ability to get into Declan's private account. The only people I know who could do that work for MacKenzie Security."

"What are you talking about? What happened?"

She turned around, and he thought she was going to run in the other direction, but she stood there staring into the night.

"Elena, why won't you talk to me? I'm your friend. I've always been your friend. You can trust me with your life."

She nodded and he watched as she physically tried to get herself under control. He'd never seen her like this. It was clear someone had done something horrible to her, but the question was who. The people who worked for MacKenzie Security were honorable men and women. None of them would breach Declan's account. But someone had. And that meant MacKenzie Security could have bigger problems than they thought.

* * * *

Elena was anxious to respond to the message. It would take more than one line to smoke out a rat. Besides, why in the world would the cartel ever imagine she'd leave the United States? It didn't make any sense. The MacKenzies had killed Alexander Ramos and the cartel had disbanded.

She couldn't trust herself. Whoever had sent the message had known exactly the right button to push to make her lose control. If it really was the cartel, they'd intercepted Declan's transmissions and taken over his server.

"Elena?" Brady said. "Have you heard one word I said?"

"I'm sorry, Brady. I've just got too much on my mind." Her chest heaved and her knees were shaking. So much for spending all those years building her strength and training. At the first sign of her past coming back to haunt her, she was nothing but weak. "You should just go back to whatever you were doing. I'm fine. I need to be alone right now. You're crowding me."

She barely caught the hurt that flashed in his eyes. And then he stiffened.

"Sure, no problem," he said. "I'll give you your space. Didn't know I'd been crowding you."

Brady slipped off the pavement and disappeared into the night without a sound, every inch the lethal warrior. Her heart ached. She'd just hurt the one true friend she really had. But the MacKenzies had risked enough for her. If it really was the cartel trying to get in touch with her, she had to keep it a secret. They were too dangerous, and she'd be damned if she put any other lives at stake.

Her mind spun back to the message. It was bait. She knew it and she also knew better than to bite. But it was eating away at her. If it was Declan, then she'd have her say. If it was the cartel, then she'd deal with it somehow. Either option sucked, but she had to know. She pulled out her cell phone and opened the encrypted message.

Time to come home, puta.

Her belly clenched again, but she willed herself not to be sick this time. Her hands were steady as she typed a reply.

I thought I was home.

Her head snapped up and she looked out into the darkness of the trees, where she expected to see the whites of eyes staring back at her. What if they were watching for her reaction? A cold spike of fear snaked its way up her spine to her scalp, the tingling almost unbearable.

"Get a grip, Elena."

She hurried back to her cabin, tightening the grip on her duffel. It had been foolish to try to leave the compound right then. An emotional reaction, not well thought out. Besides, Brady wouldn't have let her leave.

She locked the door and tugged down the shades, tossing her smartphone and duffel on the table and quickly dimming the lights. A thick quilt was folded over the back of the sofa and she grabbed it, wrapping it around her shivering body. Her teeth chattered and her skin was chilled.

She'd lived on the complex since arriving in America. Besides her niece, who lived in a Catholic convent outside of Mexico City, she had no other family. The compound was so vast that all full-time employees had cabins on the property, and there were guest cabins for the frequent visitors.

Declan had never been convinced the cartel wouldn't re-form, and if they did, the MacKenzies would be on their list for revenge. Even in the heartland of the United States, the cartel's tentacles stretched far beyond its borders. So security was tight at the compound, but that fact didn't do anything to alleviate her fear.

Her phone buzzed and she froze in surprise. The rustic décor of the mountain cabin featured a heavy copper-topped coffee table, and the sound of bouncing hard plastic resonated throughout the open-air space.

"Damn it," she said. "Jumping at shadows."

The shivering got so bad her eyes grew heavy. Maybe she could get a little sleep. She pulled her long, black hair into a ponytail and kicked her shoes across the heated floor.

The smartphone buzzed again, but she was too comfortable to bother getting up to grab it. She knew it was wrong, but she'd seen Brady's number pop up, and she just didn't have the emotional reserves to engage. Guilt gnawed at her.

She wished she could feel what she should feel when a man

like Brady showed her the kind of kindness and attention he had. The cartel had stripped her of the ability to be vulnerable. She was ashamed of her body and the horrible things they'd done to her, of the scars that were a constant reminder. She felt unworthy to even offer herself to another person. How could he ever understand what she'd gone through?

Her shivering was so violent the couch was shaking, and she tried to let out a breath of annoyance, but her teeth were chattering too hard. She tossed the quilt aside and moved to the thermostat, feeling ridiculous for turning on the heat in the middle of July.

The phone continued to buzz, but she ignored it and moved to the kitchen. She uncorked a bottle of red wine and poured it into a wide-bowled glass.

"Persistent much?" she asked, rolling her eyes.

She snatched up the phone and folded herself back into the over-stuffed chair, thumbing through emails and social media messages and ignoring the texts that were collecting.

Again, her heart ached that there was no word from the Merca team outside of Somalia. She did reply to Willa's email update on the locations secured for Declan and crew to base their operations.

The phone buzzed again, and she noticed it was another encrypted message.

Your home is here. With us. Do you miss us, puta?

She set the crystal glass on the rustic-looking coffee table. The liquid swished close to the top but didn't spill. She needed a plan of action. The fact remained that these messages were coming from Declan's account. An account that had top security clearance.

It seemed like her welcome had worn out. If not with Declan, then with someone who had access to his account. She guzzled the half-glass of merlot, feeling the warmth permeate her body.

"Screw this," she said, emboldened, and started typing.

Okay, I get the hint. I quit

She couldn't stop the tears. Her anger wasn't enough to forget the kindness and love the entire MacKenzie family and crew had shown her from the very moment they rescued her. It would be tough, but she'd been through tougher and survived.

You cannot quit. We've not begun.

The quick response chilled her blood. Elena glanced around the room before jumping up to skirt back to the front door to make sure it was locked. It was. She emptied the remaining merlot into her glass. Her nerves were frayed, but she wanted the release.

What the hell was going on? That was definitely not something Declan, or any of the MacKenzies, would ever say. Angry with her or not, they cared about others. It had to be a hacker, she thought.

"Probably some geeky teenager." Though that wouldn't explain how they knew what the cartel had done to her.

I've had enough of this game. Drop dead, she furiously typed out.

Dropping dead is not an option, puta.

Oh yeah, why not? Elena replied.

Whoever was on the other end of the message sent an image file, and her finger shook as she clicked it. And when the familiar picture came into view, nausea roiled in her belly and her wine glass dropped to the floor.

She recognized the dusty, trash-filled alleyway. The rundown shacks that lined each side and the dumpster that reeked of rotten food. She blinked, trying to clear the image, but the picture was still there.

Seeing it brought her back, taking her down a long, dark tunnel she wasn't sure she'd be able to escape from again. The first backhand had had her seeing stars, and the punch to her abdomen had doubled her over with pain. They'd ripped at her clothes while she'd tried desperately to take a breath, and when she'd finally been able to suck in air, someone had hit her again, taking her to her knees.

Blood had pooled in her mouth as she'd knelt in the dirt like a dog, fear and disbelief smothering her as the men had circled around her. She'd never forget the sound of the leather belt sliding through belt loops. Never forget the feel of the first sting as the leather struck her back.

The man with the belt had enjoyed the pain he'd inflicted because he'd kept doing it. But even through the pain, she hadn't taken her eyes off the others. She'd been a virgin. And she'd never seen a naked man. They'd disrobed with an efficiency that let her know they weren't in a hurry. They'd known no one would interrupt them. No one touched the cartel and lived to tell about it.

Whimpers escaped her throat as they closed in on her, and she shut her eyes, shaking her head back and forth, knowing it wasn't real. She tried to move, to escape, but the flashback had hold of her and wouldn't let go. She only managed to fall from the couch onto the floor, hitting her chin on the coffee table on the way down.

She didn't know how long she lay there, reliving the horrors, but she thought her heart might explode in her chest when she saw the red hot end of the branding iron flash in front of her face.

Her right foot had wedged beneath the heavy leather chair, but her left leg and both arms were sprawled out. The cell continued to buzz, and her mind replayed every assault she'd endured during those horrible January days seven years ago.

She might have blacked out for a bit, but she was still in a dark haze. Her fingers moved to her chin and sticky wetness quickly coated them. The smell of blood was strong, and bile rose in her throat. Her left hand pressed into the carpet, trying to escape—though she didn't know from what—and jagged shards of shattered glass sliced into her palm.

Something pounded against her door, and then the knob rattled. She tried moving her head to see what was happening, but her pounding skull caused her to groan in agony. She couldn't move, her body paralyzed with fear.

The continuous pounding caused the phone to tumble onto her stomach and she screamed out before tossing the blood-soaked device across the room.

The thick oak door splintered.

Elena felt the rush of warm air flood over her as the evening spilled in. She thought she heard Brady yell her name, but she couldn't be sure with the blood rushing in her ears. The thick sole of his boot crushed part of her broken wine glass into fine crystals, and he knelt down beside her.

"Oh, baby," he said. "You're hurt. What happened?"

His eyes scanned the cabin's interior, and she knew he was looking for a possible threat.

She tried to speak, but the words didn't come. She was still gasping for air.

"Take it easy," he said. "Focus on breathing. In and out." His voice was soothing—hypnotic—and he kept his gaze steadily on hers until she got herself under control.

"I...I fell out of the chair," she finally managed to get out.

"We can go with that for now," he said. "You're shivering." He pulled the thick quilt from the couch and covered her with it. "Elena, I need you to focus on me, okay?"

His voice calmed her and she just kept looking into the green depths of his eyes. There was compassion there. And worry. But he was with her, and that's what mattered.

"I'm going to have to touch you," he said. "I don't want to scare you. Tell me when you're ready, okay?"

"I...I'm okay," she stuttered, teeth chattering.

"No, baby, but you will be. Hold tight." He moved slowly so she could see what he was doing and put his arms beneath her. He lifted her from the rug and stood to his full height. Any other time, she would've been impressed by his strength.

He set her gently in the chair, and she realized she was still crying. She couldn't seem to stop the tears from streaming down her face. Brady left her and went to the kitchen, and she heard him digging through her drawers. When he came back, he knelt down in front of her, holding a damp towel. He held it gently to her chin, pressing slightly to stop the bleeding, and using his other hand to wipe the wetness from her cheeks.

"You need stitches," he said, removing the towel to check the cut.

"No, it'll be fine. I've got some super glue in the bathroom." She tried to push his hands away so she could get up, but he blocked her. It was becoming more and more imperative that she get the hell out of Surrender, Montana, as fast as she could. They'd found her. She had to run. Had to hide.

"I've got to get out of here," she said. "I can't stay here any longer. Let me go."

She tried to get to her feet again, but she was too weak. She could barely lift her arms.

"Baby, I don't know what's going on, but you're out of your mind if you think I'm going to let you leave here in this condition. You need a doctor. You've got cuts on your hands and wrist from the wine glass. And you're in shock. Your pupils are dilated and you're shaking. Your skin is cold to the touch. You need to talk to me. Were you attacked?"

She shook her head, but averted her eyes. How could she answer that? She hadn't been attacked in the here and now. But it *had* been an attack. And it had felt as real as it had seven years ago.

"I see," he said, as if he'd read her mind. "I'll call Thomas."

"No," she said, grasping his arm. "I can't deal with any more MacKenzies." Not until she found out for sure what was happening with Declan's secure account.

Brady pulled back. "I don't understand what's going on here, Elena. The MacKenzies have always been there for you. Sure, Declan's a little pissed at what happened with Alpha Team, but he'd never betray you or do you wrong. He's a good man."

She turned her head from his piercing gaze. "All I can trust is what I see with my own eyes. You'll never understand. Just leave me alone." Her voice rose in volume, but broke, lessening the impact of the order. "I have to go," she repeated. She pressed both palms into her temples and rocked back and forth. The tears wouldn't subside. Why had she thought she could live a normal life? Coming to Surrender had only been running from what she'd feared most. And, as she was finding out, what she feared would eventually catch up with her.

"I am first and foremost your friend," he told her. "I've always been your friend, even when you didn't want it. I will not leave you alone. We're your family."

The finality in his voice had her closing her eyes. She just wanted to curl into a ball and sleep forever. Maybe she could. Brady disappeared and came back a couple of minutes later with more clean hand towels and her cell phone. Her heart sank.

"Please don't do this," she said. "I'm fine. I have to go." Her head and limbs were so heavy she could barely sit upright in the chair. She couldn't even seem to keep her eyes open.

There were tears in his eyes when he lifted his phone to his ear. "I'm sorry, baby. But it's for your own good."

Her head lolled back on the chair in defeat and she let exhaustion take her.

Chapter Four

More than twenty-hours passed before she opened her eyes to glaring sunlight peeking between the slatted blinds.

She was groggy, almost hungover, and it took a minute for her eyes to adjust. She recognized the secured facility that housed the MacKenzie hospital and R&D labs. She hated hospitals, despite the fact that there was no better in the world than the facility she was in. The machine she was hooked up to started beeping faster as panic took hold of her. The memories she had of hospitals weren't good.

Her memories of the night before were fuzzy. She remembered the flashback. More vivid and intense than any she'd experienced in years. It had caught her totally off guard, and she'd crumbled as if it had been the first time. She remembered Brady, and she vaguely remembered Thomas MacKenzie arriving. He'd said she was in shock and that her vitals were out of control. Then she remembered nothing.

She felt for the bandages beneath her chin, her IV pulling in the crook of her arm. Her right wrist and arm were covered in bandages, and she seemed to be connected to every machine possible with a tangle of wires.

"Let me out of here," she said, trying to lift up to a sitting position.

She collapsed back against her pillow, shaky and weak. Whatever drugs she'd been given were making her lethargic. And she had a hell of a headache. Her hand at the side of the bed reached for the remote, and she hit the nurse call button.

"You rang?" Lacey MacKenzie said, coming in with a chart in hand. "I was wondering when you were going to wake up. You obviously needed the sleep."

"I was drugged," Elena said. "Not exactly a refreshing night's rest."

"It was nothing but a local," Lacey said. "Combined with your overall exhaustion, though, you probably feel like you've been run over by a truck."

"I've got a hell of a headache."

"You've got to take better care of yourself. Why haven't you told anyone you're having nightmares and flashbacks? If you think PTSD is something only cops and soldiers suffer from, you'd be wrong. What happened to you before isn't something that's just going to go away if you don't deal with it."

"I've dealt with it," Elena said stiffly. "My body healed. I went to counseling. Now I really need to get out of here."

"Elena…" Lacey said softly.

"I don't need your pity," Elena said. "Just let me out. I've got a million things to do."

Lacey arched a brow and crossed her arms over her chest. "You've known me a long time. I wouldn't say pity was part of my makeup. Compassion? Yes. But not pity. I didn't pity Shane while he busted his ass to walk again. You think I'm going to pity you because you've worked yourself into exhaustion and you've got a busted chin? Sister, please. That doesn't mean I can't hurt for you because I can see the torment you're going through. We can all see it. But you've never let any of us close enough to try and help you heal."

"What am I supposed to say?" Elena asked, feeling the tears threaten to fall. "How can I not remember what they made of me? Every time I look at my body, the marks are there. They made sure I'd never forget. And I can't. No amount of help from anyone is going to change that."

"I don't believe that. The people here love you. But you've done nothing but stonewall and reject us."

"I need to go," Elena whispered. Why couldn't they understand that she'd had no choice? Why would she let them in so they could feel the same horrors she felt on a daily basis? She wouldn't wish that on her worst enemy. And especially not on the people she cared about. No, it was better to keep her wall up than expose them to the memories she kept locked away. Even if they didn't understand that this was her way of protecting them.

"You're free to go, Elena. And not that you'll listen to doctor's orders, but you need to take a few days off. I've got a couple of prescriptions for you. Something that'll help with the anxiety and something that'll help you get caught up on sleep. You can take Tylenol for the headache. A nurse will be in to take out your IV and disconnect you from everything. We gave you several bags of fluids. You were dehydrated. Brady brought you some clean clothes," Lacey said, pointing to the chair in the corner. Then she walked out without looking backward.

As it should be.

"Shit," Elena said, trying to take her mind off of the friend she'd just lost. Could she have embarrassed herself in front of Brady more than she already had?

Everything was too much, just building and building inside of her, and she felt like her skin was being stretched to the point it would eventually burst open.

There was a knock on the door and her head snapped up.

"I hear they're springing you," Brady said, entering the room tentatively. His smile was strained.

"Yeah," she said. "I don't suppose you could give me a ride out of this place?"

"I'm at your service," he said. "That's the great thing about leave time. I can do what the hell I want, when I want to do it."

Her head pounded. She only knew one thing for sure and that was that the cartel had found her. It was the only possible explanation for the photos that were sent. No one who worked for MacKenzie Security would have done something so cruel, and she felt shame that even for a second she'd had the thought that they had.

She'd been alone for so long she didn't even know how to approach the topic of what had happened the night before, but Brady didn't give her the opportunity to try.

"While we're waiting for them to unhook you, it seems like a good time to talk about what I saw on your phone last night. How long has this been going on? And why the hell didn't you tell anyone?"

She could see the anger in him now. How had she not noticed he'd been concealing it when he'd first come in?

Her shoulders stiffened at the reminder of what he would've seen on her phone. It was hard for her to see it. She'd been unrecognizable as a human.

"I don't want to talk about it," she said.

"Fine. Whatever you want."

"Really?" she asked, skepticism lacing her voice. She pushed herself upright a little more, stronger than she'd been after first waking up. "You'll let it go? Just like that?"

He was still angry, but he approached her slowly, sitting on the edge of the bed. She knew deep down that Brady would never hurt her. He'd earned her trust over the years, but she didn't know how to show him that she trusted him. She didn't know how to extend an olive branch and accept his friendship—any of the friendships she'd been offered. She just wasn't equipped to deal with the emotional aspect that bringing other people into her life would entail.

"Yeah, just like that," he said. "I've tiptoed around you these last years. My heart breaks for you every damned day, and you have no idea the guilt I feel right now because I thought every last one of those bastards that had touched you was dead. We hunted them. But we clearly missed someone, or several someones.

"I'm not afraid to admit that you scare the hell out of me on some levels. I enjoy being with you. When you don't have that stick up your ass, you're fun and funny. I've overheard you joking around with Willa and a couple of the other girls, but only when your guard is down.

"I've done everything in my power to make you feel comfortable around me, but I've never had the courage to be the kind of friend where you could tell me about that night. Or the courage to listen. I do remember what it was like when we found you, and I've never been the same. I'd met you before, when you came to us with the intel, and I'd be lying if I said I hadn't been thinking about those few flirtatious exchanges we'd had. I think how things would've been different if we'd brought you into protection instead of letting you go home."

Her heart almost stopped in her chest at the anguish in his voice. She'd forgotten about that initial attraction between them—hadn't let herself remember those times.

"Brady, no, it wasn't anyone's fault but the men responsible for raping me." She wanted to reach out to him, and her hand moved, but she stopped just short of touching him and let her hand fall back to the bed.

"I just don't know what to do anymore, Elena. It's driving me crazy. We've had these moments over the years…these moments where we just…connect. I know you feel it too because that's usually when you get scared and get that stick back up your ass."

Her lips twitched at that because she knew it was true.

"I saw that shit on your cell last night, and I was so fucking pissed. And at the same time it was everything I could do not to take you in my arms and just hold you until the nightmares went away."

"You can't understand, Brady. This is my burden. No one else can carry it."

"Are you fucking serious?" he said. "I can't understand? After all the hell I've experienced in my life with the SEALs, seeing you in that street is still the hardest thing I've ever had to deal with. My heart broke that day, and it'll remain in pieces until I know yours is healed." He opened the door but glared back at her. "I've been your friend through all of this. Don't insult me like that. I deserve better. I'll wait out here until the nurse releases you. Just think about it, Elena."

A tightness settled over her chest when he walked away. She could feel the fragile threads of the life she'd been weaving together over the last seven years start to unravel. She needed help. And asking for it was the hardest thing she could ever do.

* * * *

The car ride back to the MacKenzie compound was made in silence. When they approached the massive gates, Brady typed in the code and scanned his thumbprint on the metal plate, and then the gates opened and they drove through. Brady nodded at the guards on duty.

He took the path away from the main houses, where the MacKenzies had made their homes, and toward the smattering of cabins and HQ. He parked the Jeep in front of her house and left it running, and then he got out and unlocked her front door for her.

She was steadier on her feet and followed him up the stairs and into the small space. It was just a one-bedroom cabin, with a single bath and living room and kitchen. It was all she needed. Brady did a quick walk-through to make sure everything was okay and then went back out onto the porch.

"I've got some errands to run," he said, putting on his sunglasses and getting back into the Jeep. He drove off, leaving her standing there on the threshold.

"I guess he's still pissed," she said, watching the back of the Jeep disappear down the road.

She noticed the door had been replaced where he'd kicked it in and she shut and locked it behind her. Looking around the room, it was as if nothing unusual had happened the night before. The rug had been cleaned and the glass removed. Brady did deserve so much more—but she feared she wasn't the one to give it to him.

There was one item missing from the coffee table—her cell phone. She needed that cell phone. Staying in contact was priority. She looked on the kitchen counters and then went into the bedroom, breathing a sigh of relief when she saw the phone on her bedside table. Next to it was a sticky note with one word written on it—*sleep*.

It sounded like a good idea and she smiled at the thoughtfulness. She crawled onto the mattress and let herself sink in. It was a welcome relief from the hospital bed. Her body ached, and whatever was left over in her system was making her sleepy. The nurse had given her the two prescription bottles before she'd left, but she was determined not to take them. She'd tried medicating the pain while she'd been in therapy, and the drugs had only made the nightmares worse, keeping her inside the private hell of her sleep so she couldn't wake up.

Elena pulled the covers over her and curled to her side. She wasn't sure what to do next, but one thing she did know was that she was indeed secure on the MacKenzies' complex. Even if the cartel tried to snatch her back, they'd never breach the world-class security systems or trained warriors who lived and worked on site.

Emboldened by the thought, she reached for her phone on the nightstand. She activated the Cryptocat app and jabbed at the keys to show the cartel she wouldn't fall for their intimidation tricks. She was tired of being the prey.

Go play your games with someone else. I'm through with this. Don't contact me again.

She waited almost twenty minutes for a reply. Maybe they'd grown tired of the cat and mouse charade. She fell asleep with that thought on her mind. But then the familiar buzz against her chest woke her. She held up the phone so she could see their reply.

Wrong. Game is just beginning. Time to come home, puta. You know where to find us. We never went far from home.

The cartel had acquired one of the largest Mayan temples from the *federales* through bribes and intimidation. The majestic symbol of a once great civilization now represented nothing more than a fortified drug den and whorehouse.

I am home. I'll never play with you, and I'll die before I go back into that hell.

A slight hint of confidence poked its head through her response. Maybe it was the thirty-four hundred miles separating them, but she felt a strength she hadn't felt in a long time.

Big mistake, puta. You may not play. But she will…

A sob tore from Elena's throat as the image came on screen. It was black and white, captured from a surveillance camera. But the young woman strapped to the floor was clear to see.

She'd not seen the girl since she was a child, but they'd stayed in contact over the years. So she knew without a doubt that it was Marguerite on the floor, the coif and wimple of the nun's headdress stark white in comparison to the black habit she wore. She was barely twenty, and if someone didn't do something, her life would be irrevocably changed.

After the cartel had killed Elena's father and brutalized her,

Marguerite had been sent to a convent by her uncle to make sure she was protected from retaliation. It had been a wise decision, because her uncle had been gunned down only days later.

The Sisters of Our Immaculate Conception was an obscure sect of the larger Mexico City diocese. Her niece had taken the Christian name of Marguerite instead of her given name of Maria Nayal, and the ancient convent was so far removed from civilization that even Declan felt she'd be safe.

Whatever it was that the cartel wanted from Elena, they'd shown there were no limits to reaching out to her. They had already murdered her father, a renowned scientist, so what could they possibly want now? There were no notes or passcodes left behind by her dad, so to them she had only been a toy to feast upon.

She typed out a response, begging them not to touch Marguerite, but stopped before sending it. She recalled what the MacKenzies had taught her about crisis communications and negotiations. It was vital to remain calm and appear to be in control. Otherwise, the opposition knew you were emotionally desperate and vulnerable to any demand. Elena ran her hands through her hair.

Why would you do this? What do you want?

She sat up and waited for a response. A bottle of water sat on the nightstand, but her hands trembled so violently that she couldn't hold it. Wide-eyed, Elena scanned the room for anything to help her think through the scenario.

"Fuck," she yelled, fury coursing through her body.

She threw the water bottle as hard as she could and it hit the wall, her breath heaving. She couldn't keep lying down. She had to move.

Her feet swung to the floor and she stood unsteadily and then walked into the living room. The headache was back in full force, and she dug in the little bag she'd gotten from the hospital until she found the Tylenol.

She waited for another response…and kept waiting…but there was nothing but silence and the haunting image they'd sent of her niece.

She heard a light tap on wood, and she jerked around, looking for the source. She checked her cell for a reply, but there was none. Confused, she looked around the room. The knock came again, but a little harder this time.

She laughed and shook her head, putting her hand to her racing heart. She was losing her mind. Someone was at the door. Her first temptation was to ignore it, but she remembered Brady's words from before and forced herself to look through the peephole. It had taken longer to make her decision than she'd thought because Brady was already in his Jeep and driving away by the time she found the courage to open the door.

Her pocket vibrated and she grabbed the phone. More than two hours had passed without a word. Mind games…they were great at them. She couldn't let them keep shaking her.

Time to pay up, puta. You want your niece left in one piece. We want the data.

"Data," she said. "What data? I don't have anything."

Data? she questioned.

Don't play stupid. You work for one of the most powerful companies in the world. We want access to the MacKenzie network. The data you scrape for us will be worth millions. It seems fair, considering the data was stolen from us when our network was hacked into.

Elena rested her head against the wall. Her mind reeled at the reality of their request. The MacKenzie records management system, or RMS, held top-secret-level government information. The security company Declan singlehandedly built managed many off-the-books missions the government couldn't afford to be associated with. There was no way she'd compromise every covert security operative's identity.

Impossible, she answered.

There was no delay in their response now. *Nothing is impossible. Impossible means your niece will experience your nightmares. We have shown her the video. She seemed suitably horrified. Did you know there was a video?*

"Oh God," Elena said, collapsing onto the couch. "Oh God, oh God. Why?"

Her hands shook as she typed her answer. Surely, they could see reason. *I do not have access to the network. My security clearance is low level. Let Marguerite go. Your fight is with me. She is innocent.*

There are no innocents in war, and she is no different. But what can you do? You don't have access to the network. Too bad. She's lovely.

Her gut knotted into a violent twist of pain. What was she going to do? There was only one option that she could see.

I will try, she said.

Try hard. And while you're trying, make sure you delete any intel the MacKenzies have collected on us from the hacked files. In the meantime, we'll get to know Marguerite a little better. We wonder what the stripes of our belts will look like across her back.

Elena growled in fury.

Do not touch her, she demanded. *Promise you will not touch her.*

Data first.

This will take time.

Then we will take our time with her. Better hurry.

Elena's head began to spin. She fell to her knees and fumbled to crawl toward the door. She had to get out—to escape.

She got to her feet and stumbled toward the door. Her wrist stung and she realized she must have torn her stitches at some point. Red seeped through the white bandage, but she didn't care who saw her. Marguerite was innocent, and had to be saved. So Elena gathered her strength, grabbed her ID card, and orientated herself toward headquarters.

Then she ran.

She fumbled for the plastic swipe card that activated the

biometric finger and eye scan. It was the only way she could access the tight security in the company's headquarters. Pressing her forefinger against the shirt's hem to wipe off as much blood as possible, she jammed her finger onto the crystal blue-colored rectangle. After the third error notice, it activated the retinal scan function.

Elena blinked back tears and sweat before laying her cheek against the pad. Holding her eyelid open as the light flashed across her pupil, she exhaled when she heard the lock deactivation and saw the blinking green light that signaled it was okay to enter the foyer.

From that security point, it was just a matter of using her identification badge to access each interior door. The white plastic rectangle with her photograph and a bar code dangled from a zip cord attached to her shirt. As she began to calm from her sprint across the compound, her mind continued to run scenarios for accessing the data without actually compromising anything.

"It can't be done," she muttered.

"What can't be done?"

She screamed in surprise and her knees buckled. "Brady," she panted. "What are you doing in here?"

"I'm pretty sure I'm the one who should be asking that question."

"I work here," she said hotly, her cheeks burning after being caught. "Which is more than I can say for you."

"I believe I've been on the MacKenzie payroll more than enough to qualify," he said. "You should know. You worked the boards for several of our missions. And I can take a hint. I probably should've taken it a long time ago, but I've got a head like a rock. At least that's what my mama always told me. See you around."

Chapter Five

Elena threw herself into one of the office chairs. She had to hook a toe beneath the desk to stop it from rolling into the credenza. She felt bad about lying to Brady, but this was family—her family.

Her phone buzzed and she hunched forward, reading the text.

Has it been transmitted?

She checked the security cameras and then latched the door from the inside so there were no more surprises.

There was no way she'd transfer that amount of data over the web. MacKenzie Security's fail-safe system or the federal government's classified document transmittal protection service would detect it and shut it down. Within seconds, all fingers would be pointed at her. Besides, she didn't trust the cartel to release her niece if the data went through anyway.

I'll send once she's released, Elena typed.

She instantly regretted it. They weren't a group to be intimidated or told what to do. In fact, they'd usually counter out of spite. They had no issue with hacking off their own damn nose to spite their crooked face. Honor meant nothing to them.

No

Elena dabbled with the RMS and considered a partial data

scrape. Even if she tried to mail it to them, the only portable device small enough to avoid detection was a HyperX flash drive. It only held one terabyte of data, which was a huge amount compared to anything else. Without using a portable hard drive, which would store up to three terabytes, it looked like her options were limited.

Still, even if she could run a data pipeline directly into their mainframe, the issue wasn't capacity. It was trust, and they simply could not be trusted to release her niece.

There was also the problem of the cartel's demand that she wipe all of the data seized from them by a team of MacKenzie Security specialists a few years ago. The cartel had been hacked by this crack squad of warriors and geeks. They knew that the MacKenzie's RMS held very sensitive information detailing their offshore and secret bank accounts, names of public and elected officials on the take, and names of people executed along with the location of their corpses.

The network breach had caused the cartel years of turmoil and millions of dollars in lost revenue. They attempted to backtrack and relocate all of the dead. They transferred billions of dollars, but lost millions to fees and US investigators seizing liquid assets during the transfers. The cartel had even gone as far as killing the key corrupt officials on their list to prevent the American government from interrogating them for intelligence in exchange for leniency.

Elena knew she found herself in over her head, but she had a choice that was simple—save her niece or let her be tortured and possibly killed. It was something she'd have to do on her own. No one, not even Brady, would understand her predicament. It would be the right time to react since everyone was understandably focused on the missing team in Somalia. But how?

Waiting

She slapped the cell phone screen down. Those pricks were

now toying with her. It was a tactic she'd been taught by the security specialists to create an emotional reaction to their stimuli. She wouldn't fall for it, but she couldn't allow the cartel to think she was weak or defiant. Negotiations for the life of another were often wrought with small doses of logic and huge gambles on intuition.

Network too tight. Data too big to send

She tapped her fingernails against the tabletop and prayed her gamble paid off.

Bullshit

"Dammit," she said. "I guess that means we're going for the exchange."

* * * *

The communications center was starting to feel like a box. The walls seemed to move inward the longer she was in the room, and she felt like she was suffocating. She'd been quiet and distant all morning, and even Willa's bubbly personality couldn't break her out of the funk. There was plenty of work to do so they didn't have to communicate or cross paths.

"Take five," she told Willa once the confinement had become unbearable.

Willa shrugged. "Whatever you say, boss. I don't suppose you're going to tell me what diced you up? Were you in some kind of accident?"

"Yeah," Elena said. "An accident. I cut myself shaving. I'm fine."

"Funny," Willa said. "You look like you need to be flat on your back, watching soap operas for a couple of days with one of those big ice packs on your face. Let me know if you need some relief." She looked at the clock and swore. "I've got to hurry. The SEALs usually take a run around the lake with their shirts off about this time."

"Take twenty," Elena said.

"Now you're talking." Willa waved and headed out to watch the SEALs.

Elena switched screen number three to a heads' up display that fed the entrance cameras into her view. There'd be no way she could afford to allow Brady to sneak up on her. For what she was about to begin, even Willa had to be guarded against.

She set to work creating a false data set. While it would initially appear legitimate, once inspected, the one terabyte flash drive would instead inject an unstoppable, killer Trojan virus into the cartel's information network. Within a matter of hours, the flash drive's program would transfer all new data compiled by the cartel to the MacKenzie and United States Department of Justice's shared security portal. It would effectively shut them down.

The virus, known as a cannibal virus, had been discovered during an operation in Tehran a year ago, and it was so potent that Declan felt it best contained on a separate, secure server within the vaults at MacKenzie Security headquarters. The computer attacking program would not only launch an external feed of data to a receiving source, but as it processed that data from within its host network, it permanently destroyed everything it touched.

Elena knew the consequence would be her death, but once Marguerite was safe inside the United States, she didn't care what they did to her. She even considered concealing a suicide pill just to screw the cartel out of the satisfaction of killing her.

She clicked away on computer keys and swiped furiously at touch screens to scroll through millions of bytes of data. It was vital she replicate the exact ones to fool the cartel into believing her source codes were legitimate. She knew they'd never accept the flash drive and waltz it into their mainframe's CPU. They'd demand a sample. That was when she'd secure Marguerite's release. The timing would have to be perfect.

Elena dialed down to the airfield controller's office. She told them she'd be there within the half hour. She quickly transferred her contrived data onto a disposable flash drive before combining it with the cannibal virus on the separate computer server in the technology vault in the HQ's basement. She knew accessing the vault would leave an audit trail, but she wasn't concerned. By the time anyone discovered her breach, she'd be gone—and possibly dead.

The lethal data concoction would take about two hours to process, so she'd head over to the airport hangar. Once there, she'd snatch a transport to Cancun. Like the vault access, her audit trail would be detected through the flight plan, but by then, she'd be on the ground and moving.

Elena took a golf cart to the opposite side of the compound to the private hangars and runway that housed millions of dollars of aviation equipment and aircraft. There were three large metal hangars, but one of the planes sat just outside of it.

She recognized Mira Black even from a distance. There weren't many six-foot-tall Norwegian female fighter pilots. Her white-blonde hair was braided down her back, and she somehow managed to make the shapeless coveralls look very shapely.

"Damn, girl. What the hell happened to you?" Mira asked.

"Just another day at the office," Elena said.

"I didn't have days at the office like that when I was flying missions with the Marines," Mira shot back.

"I'm fine," Elena assured her. "It looks a lot worse than it is."

"Good, because it looks pretty bad. So what can I do for you besides call a medic?"

"Before I say anything, I need to know I can trust you."

Mira looked surprised. Elena didn't make it a practice of confiding in anyone, and Mira must've known it by the look on her face. She tried not to feel guilty for playing on those emotions.

"You can trust me," Mira said. "What is it?"

"I need a quick trip to Cancun. I have business there that will only take a day or two, tops."

"Business?" Mira asked, brows raised. "I didn't get a memo about any upcoming business trips. You know I've got to complete a detailed flight plan. What kind of business? There's nothing on my schedule except a recreational skydive later on today."

Elena wasn't sure where she found the will to smile and bluster her way through, but she managed. "Okay, you got me." She raised her hands in surrender. "I just need a break, and I figured my homeland would help recharge my batteries. Declan has never had a problem with employees using the jet for vacation time, but there's a two-month request period. I wasn't planning on time off, but after losing Titus and possibly his crew, I've not been the same. I can't wait the two months. I need to get out of here now." She averted her gaze.

Mira's blue eyes turned sympathetic, and she reached out to put a comforting hand on Elena's shoulder. The kindness made her feel all the more guilty.

"I heard about that," Mira said. "Tell you what. How about I create a little schedule magic and work up that flight plan? No one really looks at them anyway. When are we leaving?"

Elena checked her watch. "Text me when you've filed the flight plan. I'll be ready to go."

"Be back here in two hours," Mira said.

* * * *

Willa was at the switchboard when Elena returned to the communication center.

"By the size of your grin, I'm guessing you found your SEALs." Elena tried to sound lighthearted, but she felt sick inside. She didn't like the lies and deceptions she'd been making up recently.

"Oh, baby, did I ever." Willa's laugh was infectious. "I've got my eye on the blond one. He's got these dimples when he smiles…" Her expression went dreamy, and Elena figured she was recalling the smile in question. "He's also got these little indents just above his hips. Sweet Lord, Holy Jesus," Willa said, fanning herself.

Elena tried to smile, and she let Willa keep talking. Her time was running out. She had to get into the vault so she could get the data. Her heart hammered in her chest. Despite Willa's flightiness, she wasn't stupid. She'd wonder why Elena was in the vault, and more than likely, she'd mention it to someone.

"Has Declan sent the foreign entry and response form yet?" she asked once Willa had wound down.

Willa shrugged, "Not that I've seen."

"He said it was vital so his team could operate without foreign military interference."

"I've got no clue what you're talking about," she said. "I've got my GED and some community college under my belt, but whatever you just said is way past my understanding."

"It's only for those Godforsaken places like Somalia. You know how corrupt stuff gets down there." Elena tried to sip water from a paper cup but her hand shook so much that it plopped over the edges. "Best not to keep Declan waiting. I'm sure you'll find it. I need to go lay down. I think my shaving incident is starting to catch up to me."

Elena turned toward the door.

"Wait," Willa blurted out.

"I know you're feeling bad, but I don't have any idea what I'm looking for. Could you get it? I don't want to screw anything up."

Elena breathed a sigh of relief. "Sure, I don't mind." Her plastic identification card was in her pocket. "I don't have my access card with me." Her palms turned upward.

Willa pulled the zip cord and unlatched the base from her belt loop. "Here, take mine."

* * * *

The men's locker room inside the MacKenzies' main airfield hangar was styled after a modern-day health club. Showers, hot tubs, and a sauna also made it a favorite hangout for the guys. It was full of testosterone and lighthearted hazing. What else was expected when a pack of alpha males got together for an afternoon of skydiving?

Brady hadn't been able to relax during his time off. He thought this might help. The nine missing agents were dominating his thoughts. He was also worried about Declan and Shane, who had hurried to South Africa to meet a team of contractors. Rescuing the team of vanished warriors seemed more unlikely as the hours flew by.

"Boy, you know Claire is going to blow a gasket when she finds out you're here." Brady patted Cooper on his shoulder.

"You kidding me? I'm not going to miss my chance to show a few vacationing Navy SEALs how to jump out of a plane. Y'all will thank me for the lesson." Cooper laughed.

Brady looked over to the three active-duty SEALs. They chuckled too, though none seemed to believe they'd be outdone by a former Army Ranger. Brady wasn't so sure. Cooper maintained his skill sets. He'd gotten out of the fast-paced life of undercover work, but his time as sheriff in Surrender hadn't been all lazy days in the bakery and sitting on the front porch of his office in a rocking chair. The vast openness of Montana lent itself to a lot of drugs, most specifically meth. There were a lot of good hiding places for trailers and makeshift labs, and with big drug operations came big violence and weapons. As sheriff, the entire territory was his to oversee and they'd gotten in some pretty tense situations over the last years.

Riley stepped out of the sauna with just a towel loosely fitted around his waist. Brady held back a chuckle because he knew the mixture of a thrill-seeking archeologist amongst these military studs was going to go over like gas and fire. He just wasn't sure who'd be which.

"You serve?" Cocker, the youngest of the SEAL team, asked Riley.

"Serve what? Your head on a platter?" Riley asked good naturedly.

It was obvious he knew exactly what Cocker was asking, but Riley lived to be contrary. He'd never been in the military, or law enforcement, for that matter, but he sought risk everywhere he turned. Brady wasn't even sure if Riley knew how to parachute jump, but he was happy he'd joined the get-together.

"In the military," Cocker clarified.

"Nah, man," Riley said. "I'm just a hole digger."

Cocker scratched his shaved head. "Well, you'll be buried in a hole if you don't know what you're doing up there."

"Huh," Riley said, scratching the stubble on his face. "So you think I need a parachute?"

"Only if you want to do it twice," Cocker said, laughing.

Brady was anxious about pitting his family against his SEAL brothers. Although it wasn't a competition, no outing with the MacKenzie men ever ended without one. He knew the SEALs would soon join in.

"Riley, I thought you were off in no-man's-land with some university-funded dig site?" Brady asked.

"I was. But the grant ended, and so did the university's enthusiasm for studying twelfth century sources of social media."

"I guess Maggie was glad to have you back."

"Not really. She was looking forward to traveling out there to stay a month. I'll surprise her with a trip to make up for this."

"For this? Don't you mean that?" Brady asked.

"Nope," Riley said, grinning unrepentantly. "I'm supposed to be cleaning out the attic. Can you imagine being up in that attic in July? She must want me dead or something."

"All right, men," Brady said. "Gather around. Except for you, Riley. Go put some damned pants on, dude."

Everyone laughed and Riley shot them the middle finger before dropping his towel right there and grabbing his clothes.

Brady rolled his eyes and clapped his hands together to get their attention. "There will be multiple jumps this afternoon. Skies are crystal clear and winds are negligible. I thought we were going to have two more." Brady scanned the lobby area and peered outside.

"Looking for us?" Grant Boone's booming voice resonated from behind Brady.

"Ladies," Cooper said to Archer and Grant as they came into the locker room.

Brady was glad to see Archer was feeling better after the day before, and he looked alert and ready to roll. Archer wasn't military, but instead served the country as a CIA covert operative. It was while he'd worked as a spook that he and Declan had met and became best friends. His wife, Audrey, was former Mossad for the Israeli government, and the truth was, she was possibly as good if not better trained as a tactical operator than anyone in the room.

"Grant, you're from Detroit," Riley said with a smirk. "What the hell do you know about skydiving?"

The big, bearded badass from Motor City stood rigid. Dressed in tattered black, square-toed motorcycle boots, diesel-stained denims, and a ratty old flannel shirt, he flashed a toothy grin.

"Not a damned thing," Grant said.

Donald "Duck" Jones, another of Brady's men, looked at him with disbelief. "Grant Boone?" he asked suspiciously. "You that guy who singlehandedly took down the cartel in Detroit?"

"Yeah, why?" Grant towered over the SEAL.

Duck smiled and extended his hand. "Just wanted to say thanks. That's my hometown hellhole. You did a great job."

They shook hands.

"A lot of good it did me."

"I know you lost your job or quit or something like that, but us folks who lived there know what went down. We do owe you. I can't wait to tell my folks we jumped together."

"I really appreciate you saying that," Grant said sincerely.

"All right, let's focus. We've got a lot of work to do, and the faster we start, the more jumps we'll get in," Brady announced over the chatter.

"Work?" Duck shrugged. "I ain't here for work, LT."

"Play," Brady corrected and then laughed. "Play."

"More like it. I'm on vacation," Jonas Samuel replied.

He was the third and oldest member of Brady's SEAL team who had accompanied him to Surrender, Montana, to enjoy a bit of R&R. Brady always felt a disconnect between them. He'd served under Shane for many years, and Brady sensed Samuel had never transitioned with the new leadership.

"Y'all get your packs together and I'll find Mira."

"Mira Black, the Marine Corps pilot?" Duck asked.

"One and the same," Archer replied.

"Damn, she's fine."

Brady held his palms up. "Keep your flight suit zipped up, Duck. Focus on the jump."

He walked toward the door that led to the tarmac and into the blistering heat. The sun bounced off the concrete and burned the rubber of his soles. It was a perfect day, and he couldn't wait to get in the air.

Mira was doing a final check of the plane, and he felt the anticipation of the coming adrenaline rush coursing through his veins.

"What's our ETA, Mira?"

.Her head snapped up and her brow creased in surprise.

"Something wrong?" Brady asked.

"Why are y'all here? You didn't get the change of flight plans and pilot? Elena said she would take care of letting you know. I thought you'd given your approval."

"Why would I do that?" he asked, confused. "I scheduled this weeks ago. And I haven't seen Elena since earlier. What's going on? Is there an issue with the plane?"

"No, it's...Elena," Mira said. "I'm sorry, man. She requested a flight. Said it was really important. More of a therapeutic emergency after all the shit that happened with the group in Somalia. I felt bad for her, so I told her I'd fly her to Mexico. I knew there was a jump scheduled for this afternoon, but I was able to get Rudy to trade off with me. I didn't figure Elena would be comfortable with Rudy flying her all the way to Mexico."

"Why the hell does she want to go to Mexico?" he asked, feeling the heat rise from below his unzipped collar. It wasn't because of the July weather

"She said it was personal," Mira said, shrugging. "She just needs to go home for a while. Get away from everything that's going on here."

His jaw was like a piece of granite, his teeth clenched tightly together. "Do me a favor and go ahead and take the boys up. I'm going to find Elena and figure out what the hell is going on. I'll get back to you."

"If you ask me, the girl's got trouble. She's scared and she's trying to rabbit. Better tread lightly. She's resourceful."

Brady nodded and headed toward one of the golf carts.

Chapter Six

Elena didn't expect to return. It was a suicide mission, plain and simple. But it was worth the sacrifice if she was able to save Marguerite from the horrors she'd experienced.

She grabbed only a small bag, but would still have to get through TSA and then customs in Mexico. She knew scrutiny wasn't as tight on private jets, but there were still items required to pretend she was on vacation.

It wasn't as though she'd parachute into the jungle just outside of Calakmul. Brady and Declan, maybe. But not her. The wall clock showed she had less than fifteen minutes to meet Mira. Elena flopped onto her cozy, oversized bed one last time and closed her eyes, trying to get her thoughts together.

"Jesus, help me," she said.

"I'm glad you're at least clueing him in on what the hell you're doing."

"Brady," she said, rolling to her feet. "You scared the crap out of me. What are you doing here?"

Brady unzipped the olive-drab-colored flight suit as he approached her. It was pocked with sweat, and she could see he was already angry.

"Don't worry about what I'm doing. Where do you think you're going in my plane?"

"Your plane? Oh, so I no longer have access to air transportation?" Elena rolled her neck, preparing herself for the confrontation.

"All of a sudden you have important business in Mexico?" He pushed the dark lensed sunshades back through his shaggy blond hair. "I'm calling bullshit. You've decided to get in the middle of whatever is going on with those texts. And I'm not going to let you."

"You can call bullshit all you want, but that doesn't change the fact that this is none of your business."

"You know as well as I do that I can make sure you don't go anywhere on that plane."

"Then you can go straight to hell, Brady Scott," she said, more calmly than she felt. "Because I'm going to do exactly what I want to do."

He looked stunned.

"Maybe so," he said. "But whatever it is you're about to get into isn't going to be on my watch. You can be mad all you want, but at least you'll be alive."

"You can't stop me from leaving." She swung her purse at him. Brady leaned back, though it was nowhere near striking him. "I'm not your prisoner."

"You're free to leave any time you wish, but not in that plane. You can walk to Mexico as far as I'm concerned."

Elena snatched up her shoulder bag and stormed past Brady. "Fine."

"Yeah, fine. Have a nice walk. It's only two thousand miles."

She spun back around and opened and closed her fists, still debating the merits of taking a swing at him.

"Why are you butting into my life?" she cried. "You keep spouting all that bullshit about being my friend, and this is how you treat me? You don't even realize what you're doing, but I can guarantee you you're not being a friend. I need to leave here, and I need to leave now."

Brady kept his distance. "I'm not treating you any way, Elena. I'm treating you the same way I've treated you since we first met. I'm protecting you, when you don't have the sense or ability to do what's best for yourself." He took a step toward her. "Why don't you trust me with whatever it is that has you acting like this? I hope you know you can count on me to keep it confidential."

"I can't. I have to go alone."

She knuckled her wet eyes. Her shoulders shuddered with a few quick, intense sobs.

"Go where, Elena?"

"Brady, I can't. They'll kill her."

The tears escaped then. She couldn't hold them back. The reality of what was going to happen to Marguerite landed on her like cement. Hands trembled as she fell against Brady's chest. She felt his hesitation but he quickly held her, whispering soft assurances as he comforted her.

"Please, Elena, let me help you," he whispered against the top of her head.

She felt relief in his arms, and she knew she could trust Brady. That he was the one to help her save her niece.

"I've got to leave now, Brady. They're waiting." She moved toward the door.

"Elena, we're back to square one. Unless it's the cafeteria, you're not getting anywhere fast. Why don't you take five minutes and share with me what's going on?"

He helped her back onto the bed. Elena handed him the cell phone device with the encrypted app accessed, and she felt the wind go out of her sails. She was exhausted after the events of the last few days. She collapsed in sheer emotional fatigue. It wasn't until she lay still that the stitches in her chin and wrist began to throb again.

"Jesus, Elena," he said. "You should have come to me

immediately. To any of us. I'm so sorry, baby."

There was a hardness in his eyes, but she wasn't afraid of his anger. It was the cartel that should be afraid, because he looked like he was out for blood.

"No apologies," she said. "It's my fault. I should've never allowed her to remain in Mexico. I could've brought her here, but she seemed so happy at the convent. It's what she wanted, and she was safe there. At least I thought she was."

She felt Brady's hand stroke the back of her head. Suprisingly, his touch didn't send her scrambling across the room in a panic. She hated what the cartel had done to her and how it continued to affect her. But it would stop. Even if it cost her life.

"You could've never imagined the cartel would find her, much less that they'd know there was a connection between you two." Brady lifted Elena's shoulders to help her sit up. "Listen, let's resolve this and get her back here. I need to know everything."

Reluctantly, Elena collected herself and began the process of filling in the holes for Brady. She saw the sadness in his expression, but more importantly, she knew the wheels were turning. He'd have a plan devised before she finished her details. She trusted this honorable man. He was a warrior who'd faced and cheated death, but he was always kind, a gentleman with her. He deserved to be treated better than she had treated him.

"Brady, stop for a moment."

"What? I thought time was running out." His hands rubbed each other as thoughtful energy seemed to pulse through his body.

"This won't take long."

Elena sucked in a quick breath and felt fear wrestle with relief and anticipation. She reached across, her hands shaking, and placed her palms against the warm skin of his arm. It was as brave as she was able to get. Her gaze locked with his, and his eyes widened with surprise.

"I just wanted you to know I think you're a good man," she finally said. "I know I haven't shown it. And I'm sorry."

"You don't ever have to be sorry, Elena. I'm a patient man. And despite the fact that you've built a shell of protection around you these last years, I can still see your heart. I've watched you train and learn how to fight. I've watched you sweat out your nightmares in the gym instead of trying to sleep. And I've watched you become an incredibly strong and determined woman who I admire more than anyone I've ever known. You're beautiful, inside and out, and you're the kind of woman who wants to do the right thing, and who never wants to see anyone suffer. It's why you gave the information to Declan about the cartel years ago. Because it was the right thing to do."

"And look who suffered for it," she said, her smile sad.

"You suffered for it," he said. "But you also survived despite the suffering. You're a hell of a woman, Elena Nayal. And if we need to go kick the cartel's ass and remind them that the MacKenzies don't play, then that's what we'll do. And we'll do it together."

He leaned in and her eyes fluttered closed as his lips touched hers. It was sweet and simple—brief—but it opened up a window inside of her she thought had been nailed shut. And through that crack in the window was a gentle stirring of desire.

"Do you trust me?" he asked.

"Always," she told him.

"Good, then trust me to get Marguerite out of there. I've got a few calls to make while you repack that skimpy bag. It's got to look like we're on a honeymoon. But don't forget to pack clothes for the jungle along with your bikini," he winked.

She felt the hitch of fear in her gut but pushed it aside. She could pretend to be Brady's wife for a short time. She could get used to living in close quarters with him, having him touch her in public like husbands did with their wives.

"Done," she told him.

"And do not lose that flash drive," he said in all seriousness. "It's not only the ticket to getting her out, but it's got classified information on it."

Elena scooted off the giant mattress and went about reorganizing her carry-on bag. She stopped to listen to Brady's calls.

"Mira," he said into the speakerphone. "We're a go for Cancun. Go ahead and file a flight plan and fuel up. Tell the boys that Rudy will take them out for another jump since we need you."

"Oh, are you?" Mira said silkily into the phone. "Maybe you need me enough to tell me why the hell y'all are running around like chickens with your heads cut off and trying to keep secrets from everyone. I'm assuming Declan is going to be okay with this? Not that I can ask him right now."

Brady sighed. "He'll be fine with it. We've got a strategy in place now. We'll stop over at Miami International before hitting the Yucatan. Tell Archer he's needed too."

"Archer?" Elena asked, but Brady had already disconnected and was dialing again.

His next call was to Audrey, but they barely spoke for thirty seconds before disconnecting.

"Just like that?" she asked. "She agreed to come?"

Brady shrugged. "We need her. She has assets on the ground in Cancun and throughout the peninsula. It's going to take more than a burner and a fake flash drive."

"A burner?"

"A throwaway cell phone so we can't be traced." Brady picked up her canvas bag. "Trust me. Audrey is all business in these situations. She and Archer are the perfect cover couple. The cartel will expect you to come alone or with an army. Two couples on a vacation to a resort isn't going to raise an eyebrow."

* * * *

The clear blue Montana sky created a brilliant backdrop. Gleaming in the late afternoon sun was a spotless midsized jet, the Cessna Citation Sovereign. It was the perfect choice to get them across the country and into an international airport.

Planted in front of the pearl-colored jet with sparkling gold letters was Mira, a very irritated look on her face. She stood in the sun with her arms folded tight across her chest while her white-blonde hair fluttered in the breeze around her striking face. Brady knew he still hadn't given her the explanation she'd asked for.

"Captain," Brady said.

She sighed. "Bastard," she said good naturedly. "No need making nice. I'm here when you need me."

"I appreciate the shift in plans. It's an emergency activation. Are we all clear for takeoff?"

"Yep. Stopover in Miami and a quick refuel. You and Archer will deplane while Audrey and Elena stay tucked tight. I've already reserved a private lounge for you to meet with Chuck Magnum."

"He sounds like a porn star," Brady said, making Mira smile. "Hell, he might be for all I know, but he's also the best passport guy in the world. Oh, by the way, start calling us Robert and Julie Smith," he said. "Or you can call me Doctor Smith."

"Seriously? Doctor Smith?" Mira asked. "Hope you don't have to do emergency surgery."

Audrey and Archer came up behind them, and he heard Audrey snort out a laugh. "He'd probably try to bluster his way through it," she told Mira. "He's ballsy."

"Thank you for noticing," he said. "Let's load up."

* * * *

Elena and the team boarded the Cessna and each took a plush leather seat in the same pearl white as the outside of the plane. The carpet and interior walls were also white and trimmed with a polished oak.

Brady had changed out of the jumpsuit he'd donned for skydiving. He wore loose linen pants and a white Gauyabera shirt, and he sat across from Elena, who wore Bermuda shorts and a hideous Hawaiian flowered shirt. He winked at her as he riffled through paperwork.

"Once we hit Miami, let's get right into the lounge, finish up with Magnum, and hop over to Cancun," Brady said. "Elena, I had your passport photo from the file, so you can stay tucked in here with Audrey while we do business. Magnum isn't a fan of women."

"What about this?" she asked, holding up the short platinum wig she planned to use as her disguise. "My passport photo won't match."

"Women change their hair all the time," Audrey said. "There's a reason we're going through Miami. It's party central. And those TSA agents are used to dealing with a variety of people trying to get on a plane. They're not going to pay any attention to your picture."

Archer reached across the aisle and held his wife's hand. Elena noticed the tenderness with which he treated her. She also noticed the stitching of scars and wounds that traversed across Audrey's skin. She knew some of Audrey's story, but not all, obviously. She knew she'd been a Mossad agent who'd been captured and tortured by the Palestinians before being rescued by the Americans. And she knew she'd been shot and left to die by her lover, who'd turned out to be a terrorist double agent for the CIA. She could feel sympathy for Audrey, and she admired how she never tried to hide her scars.

"Thank you," Elena told her.

"What?" Audrey asked.

Elena pressed a palm against the corner of her eye. "Thank you for helping me. All of you. I can't tell you how much I appreciate it."

"We're sisters," Audrey said, shrugging. "As is your niece. We stick together. You and I know torture. If we can stop it from happening to someone else, then we will."

Elena took a deep breath and realized she was slowly letting them in. And it felt good.

Brady smiled her way and continued with the briefing. "We'll arrive at Cancun International and taxi to the private jet area in the far southeast corner of the airfield. It's not a very big airport, so we need to blend and get through customs as quick as possible."

"Do you think they'll be expecting her?" Archer asked.

"I'm afraid so." Elena handed over her cell phone so Audrey and Archer could see the texts.

"Damn," Audrey said. "You're going to have to take a new passport photo of her with the wig. Do we have time?"

"Unfortunately, no. But it doesn't necessarily mean they're expecting her though," Archer said. "Whoever contacted her is expecting data. That can easily be done from a remote location."

"He knows I'd come after Marguerite," Elena said. "To make sure he keeps his promise and releases her."

"You realize if you'd come alone you'd probably both end up dead?" Audrey asked.

Elena nodded. "I was hoping Marguerite would be able to get to safety."

"Damn, girl," Audrey said. "Talk about ballsy."

"That's not exactly how I'd describe a suicide mission," Brady said.

Chapter Seven

"Magnum, thank you for meeting us here," Brady greeted the husky Slovenian.

"*Zdravo*, Lieutenant Scott. Who's your friend?"

Magnum sat in the private lounge at the end of a conference table, shoveling small sandwiches into his mouth. He was shaped like a potato and his greasy hair was slicked to one side to partially hide a bald spot. The front of his white shirt had crumbs and what looked like a dab of mustard.

"I'm Archer Ryan," Archer said. "You know who I am?"

"You're the reason I'm under Declan MacKenzie's thumb," Magnum spat. "What happened to free enterprise?"

"There's no such thing as free enterprise when you align yourself with the terrorists. At least we left you alive. We don't get a thank you for that?" Archer asked sarcastically.

"*Jeba,*" Magnum said. The insult clear.

"Maybe if we have time later," Archer said, his smile cold. He stood a little taller and Magnum backed down. Archer was no one to mess with, and Magnum should remember that well. "I suggest we move on. We have places to be."

"You got the docs?" Brady asked.

Two slick-covered booklets slipped through Magnum's

fingers and onto the bar-top table. Each one was a United States passport. Brady swiped them up and examined the contents. Immaculate, with the exception of their surnames.

"Hilter? What the fuck is this? A joke?" Brady threw the documents back at Magnum. They bounced off his barrel chest and flopped onto the floor.

"I thought the name Smith was...unimaginative." His smile was sly, and he briefly flashed a silver incisor.

"I can't use these." Brady padded around the small but luxurious private lounge. He raked his fingers through his hair. "How long will it take to fix these?"

"You'll pay for these and new ones."

"How long?" Brady's voice remained low but anger simmered inside of him.

"Eight to ten hours." Magnum smacked in arrogance.

"Try again," Archer said.

"Not sure why you're pissed," Magnum said. "It's Hilter, not Hitler. Don't you see the difference?"

Brady tossed the two passports toward him. "You've got one hour to make this right."

"Not going to happen. It'll take me that long to get onto the interstate. You'll pay me for these or I'm walking out. You want new ones, then you can wait until I get done. Eight to ten hours."

Brady slapped the complimentary tray of finger foods off of the counter and pressed in toward Magnum, pulling him out of the chair by the shirt collar and shoving him against the wall.

"These only took two hours to doctor up. What's the extra time for?"

Magnum grumbled a low guttural sound as he looked Archer over from head to toe.

"Him. You brought him, that's why. Eight to ten hours."

"Fine," Brady said. "Mr. and Mrs. Hilter it is. But consider this the last time MacKenzie does business with you. How much?" Brady let go of his shirt and pulled out a wad of cash.

"Six large." Magnum's dull eyes waxed cold over the stack of bills.

"That's two grand more than you said."

"It's an administrative fee," Magnum said.

"Do you understand what it means when I say this is the last time the MacKenzies do business with you?" Brady said, his voice soft. "It means that the only reason you're alive right now is because Declan MacKenzie wants you to be alive."

Archer took the KA-BAR from his boot and started cleaning his nails with it, and Magnum's eyes darted back and forth between the knife and Brady. Sweat beaded on his upper lip.

"It means you're not going to have a nice safe place to do business anymore," he continued. "Remember what it was like to be on the run like a rat, doing dirty deals in warehouses and alleys? Remember what it was like to know you were being hunted?"

"I won't toy with you this time," Archer said. He moved swiftly and the knife embedded in the sheetrock just to the side of Magnum's face. A trickle of blood escaped from where the knife had nicked his ear, and the smell of urine was strong in the room as Magnum's bladder lost control.

"F...four thousand," he said.

"A hell of a deal," Brady said, taking the passports from Magnum and dropping the money into the urine at his feet.

* * * *

"This is go-time. Everyone remember your cover," Brady said.

Elena hunched over slightly as the jet circled the region while waiting for clearance to land. The reality of returning home had her muscles in knots and her tummy twisting flips. She drew the shade down after taking a peek through the window. The area's beauty, which attracted most visitors, repulsed her.

"You okay, Elena?" Archer asked.

Nausea swept over her as she hung her head between both knees and gave a thumbs-up.

"Hang in there. Once we go operational, you'll kick into the swing."

"Archer's right," Brady said. "You're like a machine once the go switch is flipped. Just try to stay relaxed. They'll be looking for you at the airport. No one will suspect a blonde-haired Julie Hilter. Mira, you on with us?"

"Roger that. I'm monitoring through intercom."

"Thanks. Once we land, Mira will put on her chauffeur's hat and drive us in the rented sedan to the resort. We can't afford an abduction along the way," Brady said. "Mira, once you quick clear the pilot's terminal, there will be a rental in the name of Dr. Robert Hilter."

"Roger that, boss. Glad you were able to change the name on the reservation."

"Won't they go through this jet if she leaves it in a hangar?" asked Audrey.

"They'll go through it either way. Might as well make it easy for them. This cabin has to be spotless—no clues."

"Is the cartel that embedded here?" Mira asked.

"Yes," they all said.

"Touchdown in fifteen," Mira advised.

"Okay," Brady replied. "We'll mix into the resort the rest of the day. We have a Jeep excursion scheduled before sunset tomorrow. It will give us a chance to pull off the path while the others are holding hands as the sun goes down."

"Chance for what? Aren't we're moving in tonight?" Elena asked anxiously.

"Sorry, but no. Audrey's assets on the peninsula are set to deploy two golf carts tomorrow afternoon."

"Golf carts?" she asked skeptically. "We're supposed to make our escape on golf carts?"

"Golf carts are street legal," he said, lips twitching with humor. "Besides, these have been tweaked a little. You're going to have to hold on to your ass."

"Interesting imagery," she said.

"Audrey has the coordinates, but we'll need to check the equipment they stocked the vehicles with."

"Weapons?" Archer asked.

"Yes, but for this phase we need highly encrypted covert communications and surveillance equipment."

"Why can't we just go tonight?" Elena asked. "They're getting more aggressive, and I'm worried sick about Marguerite."

"Listen, Elena," Audrey said. "We're here to help. And we'll do everything in our power to save Marguerite. But think how much closer we'd be if you'd come to us the moment this cat and mouse game started. This is the tough love portion of the trip. You don't have time to be worried, and we can't waste our energy worrying about whether or not you're going to fall apart. We're only as strong as our weakest link. Right now, that link is you. You're not a field agent but you've been a part of this organization for a lot of years. You've trained with us. You know how to fight. You know how to shoot. And you know how to keep your cool when things go to shit on the ground. I know it's different when the threat is pointed toward you. But when the enemy plays on those weaknesses, they will bring you to your knees if you let them. I've been there. We've all been there. There will be plenty of time to fall apart after it's done, okay?"

Elena knew Audrey was right. She was better than this. Stronger than this, and she hadn't worked like a dog these last seven years so she could crumble. She felt Brady's hand squeeze her shoulder in support and appreciated it more than he could know.

"Strap in for landing," Mira called out.

Elena forced herself upright as the jet eased onto the runway like hot butter on bread. She fought a panic attack as her cell phone, which had intermittently gone in and out of carrier service, began to dump messages and two missed phone calls.

"They're calling me now," she said, looking at the others.

"It shows they're desperate." Brady added, "I know this sounds harsh, but if they wanted to rape and torture someone, they could pick anyone. They grabbed Marguerite to get to you. They harm her, they lose you. They lose you and they lose the data. Therefore, they don't harm her. Get it?"

Elena breathed deep and calmed the initial panic. "I know all of that logically, but all I can think about is what they did to me. I can't stomach the thought of that happening to my niece."

The others were unbuckled and gathering their things while Elena sat frozen. She was nauseated, and it was everything she could do not to be sick. They'd sent more images, and she didn't have the courage to click on them and see whatever horrors were captured forever.

"Make a choice, Elena," Audrey said. "Either help or go back with Mira. You've got ten minutes to make up your mind or we'll make the decision for you. It's not only Marguerite's life on the line. It's all of ours. It's time to be smart and strong."

They left her alone inside the plane to make her decision, even Brady, and she finally managed to get unbuckled and stumble to the bathroom. She looked at herself in the mirror and noticed how dark her eyes looked against her pale skin. She looked sick and shaken as she removed the bandage from her chin, but she ran the cold water and splashed it on her face, reminding herself to calm down and focus.

When she went back into the cabin, she could hear the others talking outside. She knew her time was almost up. She unlocked the cell phone and clicked on the images they'd sent, bracing herself for the onslaught. The first one wasn't an image of Marguerite, as she'd feared, but of her, chained like a dog for others to pet.

"This isn't me anymore," she said, stronger than she felt. And then she deleted it. She scrolled to the next picture, and then the next, and did the same with all of them.

Elena stuffed the cell phone into her purse and hurriedly straightened her clothes and her spine. She was supposed to be enjoying her resort vacation with her husband, and by God, no one would be able to tell otherwise.

"I'm in," she said. "One hundred percent."

Brady smiled and reached up to help her down the ladder, and he let their touch linger long enough that her breath caught. Then she realized she was being foolish. They were married. And that's what married couples did. He was just acting out the part.

"Play it up in public," he whispered as he kissed her ear.

Dio, he was making her lose her mind. She fought off the shudder, completely out of her element. It was hard to remember the Elena she'd been before the attack. But those feelings Brady had incited in her were coming back with alarming speed.

She smiled coyly. "You're just trying to get away with more *besos.*" She pushed out of his arms, feeling awkward at this new dance.

"Welcome back, Julie."

"Thank you, Robert."

Archer swept Elena's canvas bag up from the cargo compartment and waved for them to move out.

Chapter Eight

"Do you mind if I ask how you got the flash drive through security?" Mira looked back at Elena through the rearview mirror.

"She slipped it into her makeup bag," Archer said.

"You saw that?" Elena asked.

"I was a spy," he said. "I see everything."

"Very funny," she said.

It was almost an hour drive to the resort from the airport, and the emotional ups and downs of the past few days were taking their toll on her. She was exhausted and dozed off and on in the back seat. The night was black and starless, and the two-lane highway dimly lit. The flash of streetlights was hypnotic.

She had removed the bandage on her chin in the airplane and examined the stitches. The wound was still red and angry looking, but there was no need for the larger bandage. She'd been able to cover it with a regular Band-Aid. The cuts on her hand and wrist weren't as serious, but she still had to be careful she didn't open anything back up.

"Wake up, baby," Brady said softly. He held her hand and rubbed gently until she was able to get rid of the sleep fog. "You need at least a solid eight hours. You've got to take care of yourself or you'll be no good to anyone."

"Believe me," she said. "A bed is what I'm most looking forward to right now, though a shower is running a close second."

"We're here," Brady said.

It was obvious they were in the tourist areas because the dark highway opened to more lanes and was brighter than the strip in Vegas. Huge stucco walls lined both sides of the road and palm trees towered, giving the illusion that paradise was just inside the gates. All of the resorts had a gatehouse and a guard, and only guests could enter the property.

Mira turned into their resort, flashed a smile at the guard and handed him everyone's passports. She dropped the rear window and, after an elderly man poked his head through a few times, they were waved on.

Elena was thankful Brady had Mira on the team. She was loyal, passionate, and although she still very much paraded her hard, Marine Corps exterior, she had a heart of gold.

The resort was opulence magnified. The main lobby was open and airy, like a palace with no walls, and no expense had been spared. There were fountains and chandeliers, and even flamingos roamed freely through the resort grounds. The main lobby was higher up than the rest of the complex, and the view out the back was beautiful. Pools and spas dotted the exterior like crystals upon a velvet cloth, and tiny villas that looked like dollhouses were lit up like Christmas. And then at the far side was a tall tower where the hotel rooms were. Even from where they stood, the crashing waves could be heard.

Elena breathed it all in, but the conflicting portrait between this and what waited for them across the peninsula wasn't lost on her. She felt awkward as they moved through the check-in process. She knew the others were watching for everything and everyone who might be working for the cartel. She only hoped to spot Marguerite. Impossible, yes, but still she hoped, no matter how unrealistic.

They were led to their rooms by two girls in tiny sarongs and bikini tops. Brady flashed a suite access card across the security reader and then they were inside. Finally, privacy from everyone other than the one person she trusted.

"You know, you really should've let me carry you across the threshold," he said.

"Sorry, maybe next time. I'm asleep on my feet."

"Man, just like an old married couple," he said incredulously.

The pout in his voice made her grin and she moved toward the bedroom. She just needed to lie down for a little while.

"I can't stop thinking about Alpha Team," Brady said. "I've heard nothing from Declan."

"I'm worried too," she said, praying those nine lives weren't lost because of her, but afraid her prayers would go unanswered.

"Hey," he said, moving toward her. She caught her breath as they stood just a hairsbreadth apart and, almost as if he were testing her, he slowly brought his arms around her in an embrace.

She shuddered at his touch. But not in fear. There were no words to describe it. When was the last time she'd felt the physical comfort of another human being? She couldn't answer the question.

"You know how Declan is," he said. "No news is good news. I'm sure he'll reach out soon."

"Does he know about this operation?" she asked.

Brady shook his head. "No. I thought it best to surprise him."

She laughed at that, knowing one thing Declan hated more than anything was surprises, especially surprises that pertained to a mission.

"Probably best. He needs to focus on Somalia."

"I don't know. He's going to be pissed. He expects me to cover for you, but he'll expect a full report from Archer.

"And I'm sure as soon as Archer is able to get hold of Declan, he'll give him one," she said. "For now, I'm just happy to see the end of this day."

Brady gently tilted her chin, "And I'm relieved that you're ending it with me by your side."

Elena looked up. She blinked back wetness in her eyes and licked her lips. His gaze followed the movement. So when he leaned down to kiss her, it seemed like the most natural thing in the world.

It was sweet—gentle—like kisses she'd dreamed of, and her heart raced as feelings she'd thought dead began to tingle through her body. She felt alive. And she felt cherished. Not worthless or used. She felt...loved. And when her mouth parted on a sigh and his tongue prodded at the opening, she welcomed him and relaxed into his embrace.

A rap against the door had his roaming hands freezing where they were. He moved her toward the bathroom and gently pushed her inside.

"Stay here," he said. "And stay quiet."

Again, there was another knock. More aggressive this time.

Brady wasn't helpless without a gun, but she knew he sure preferred the advantage one gave him. He swiped up a small, jagged rock set upon an executive mahogany desk. It was meant to be a paperweight, but Elena had no doubt it would become a weapon if need be. She wanted to peek through the crack in the door but understood the liability she'd become if things got ugly.

"Yes?" Brady called out in a commanding tone.

"Your excursion package, Dr. Hilter," a man said.

"We're kinda busy. Can you leave it by the door?"

"*Oh, si.*" Elena could hear the man's chuckle from where she was standing. "*Lo siento.*"

"Always an interruption," he said, coming back to her.

She was still flying high on the feel of his lips against hers, and she was eager to do it again. So this time, when his mouth found hers, she moaned in greeting, her fingers digging into his shoulders.

She'd been standoffish over the last years, but the patience and loyalty Brady had shown during her toughest times had convinced her she could completely trust him. And from the foreign feelings rioting through her body, she was also open to a whole host of other emotions where he was concerned.

Brady kissed her and guided her down the long hallway toward the bedroom as butterflies danced in her stomach. The master suite had French doors that separated the room from the rest of the suite and a bathroom that was almost as big as her cabin at home. Her back hit the French doors and they opened, as he pushed her inside before pulling away, the flush of arousal clear on his cheeks, his breathing strained.

"I'm about to do something very heroic," he said.

She grinned, enjoying his playfulness. "Oh, yeah?" she asked. "I can't wait to see that."

He leaned in and gave her one more kiss and then grabbed each handle of the French doors and began to pull them closed.

"Get some sleep," he smiled. "We've got a busy day tomorrow."

Elena arched a brow. "I don't know if I'd call that heroism."

"Believe me, it is," he said, and quietly shut the doors.

* * * *

Brady had been right. He was a hero because she'd felt much better when she woke the next morning. Not only that, but her body wasn't as sore and she didn't look quite so much like she'd been in the ring with Rocky.

She and Brady had been the perfect honeymooning couple for the rest of the day. They'd walked the romantic paths hand in hand, relaxed in the hot tub, enjoyed a lunch by the pool, and laid out under the sun for an afternoon nap. Then they headed back to the room to get ready for the Jeep excursion that would lead them to the golf carts so they could complete the mission.

"Can't we just go alone?" she asked when they finally broke apart from another kiss. "I'm not as comfortable with the others."

"They're here to help," he said. "Audrey doesn't take any bullshit, and she can be straightforward to the point of uncomfortable. But she's loyal, and she's one of the best covert ops agents I've ever had the privilege of watching. Be glad she's on our side. And Archer is just an up-and-up badass. I'd never tangle with him."

"You'd lose?" she asked.

"Hell no," he said. "But my body would hurt a lot, and I'm not as young as I used to be."

Brady opened the front of his hideously decorated Hawaiian flowered shirt. She marveled at the chiseled muscles and skin so tight it looked shrink-wrapped.

"Brady, I think you might draw too much attention if you go out like that," Elena said, eyeing him up and down and secretly delighting in her growing confidence.

"Oh, really? And that sheer sundress isn't going to scream out like a fire alarm?"

"We're supposed to be on our honeymoon. What else should I wear?"

Brady let out a low, long whistle. "Nothing. That's perfect."

"Let's move out," Archer yelled through the door.

"I'll sweep around and grab the excursion package," Brady said.

Even when flirting, his mind was always in operations mode. Elena had to get her focus back on why they were here. She felt the weight of her grief over her niece's capture and her sudden awakening to an incredible man who had been right in front of her eyes the entire time she'd shut herself off from the male world.

"Looks like the package left at the door is legit," Brady said. "Let's roll."

Her cell phone buzzed and Elena froze. They'd been taunting her and she'd been silent for too long. When she looked at the screen an animal sound escaped her throat and she dropped the phone. It landed face up.

They all stood, stunned and staring. The open screen showed the horrifying image. Marguerite strapped naked to an old mattress. Another image followed closely behind it and she heard Brady's ripe swear. A man holding a thick leather belt stood next to Marguerite, the terrified look on her face captured forever.

We have eyes and ears everywhere. We are the cartel. We suggest you stop whatever it is you are planning. Transmit the data now.

* * * *

The resort was full of honeymooning couples wrapped up in each other, and none of them listened to the guide as he gave instructions for the Jeep excursion to tour the island. Brady hugged Elena tight as the guide droned on about driving safety.

His thoughts drifted to the rugged terrain he'd chewed up back in Montana while putting their fleet of Jeeps to the test. He knew this drive wasn't about seeing sights or sunsets. It was about veering off the path to locate the two golf carts Audrey had secured for them to drive the three hundred and fifty miles to Xpujil. The seven-hour trek would probably take longer because they'd have to bypass checkpoints.

"Okay, happy couples. Let's hop in and crank up that engine," the Jeep guide said.

"Let's go, honey bunny," Archer said, rolling his eyes.

"If you call me that again, you're sleeping on the couch,"

Audrey said. She shoved him out of the driver's seat.

"Yeah, right," he whispered to Brady. "She loves when I call her that."

"We'll take rear guard," Brady said. "When it's time to turn off, just pop the emergency flashers on and off a few times. I'll hit my high beams to confirm." He helped Elena into the passenger's side seat.

"Whatcha doing with that?" Brady saw Elena activating her running app on the cell phone. It was a popular program for tracking the route, distance, and time it took to run courses.

She initially tried to hide it by shoving the phone beneath her thigh. Brady wasn't comfortable with her use of it because it had a global sharing feature that allowed runners to post their best runs and challenge others to match or beat them.

"I like to have a backup," she said.

"A backup?"

"What if something happens to those two overnight? It's best to have an exact route for us to follow back to the golf carts."

"I don't think it's a good idea to lay out our route on a public access app." Brady looked back and forth between her and the other Jeep.

"How about after we find the two golf carts, I delete the file? Then we'll have it committed to memory. Deal?" She rubbed Brady's arm.

He knew he was being played, but what could he do? "Deal."

Brady thought through scenarios for surviving this mission. He'd been in desperate situations before, but always with the best trained warriors on the globe. This time the reluctant but capable duo of Archer and Audrey, along with the highly volatile Elena, made him dread the hopelessness of the situation. Of course, he chuckled to himself, because he was nothing more than a love-struck pup trying to protect his lady.

"There it is. See the reflectors flashing from our headlights?"

Elena said.

Brady popped his high beam lights twice and followed Archer's bright red Wrangler onto a narrow path to the left of the main tourist trail.

"You sure you don't want to stick with the others and spend a romantic evening watching the sunset?" Brady teased.

"Later."

"Later tonight?" Brady leaned across the open console of the topless Jeep.

"Give a boy a kiss and he turns into a wild man. How about we just get through this first?"

"I keep waiting for someone to pinch me so I can wake up. I've waited for you a long time. I can wait longer."

Elena placed her hand across Brady's muscular forearm. He glanced at her as palm fronds and branches from a tropical jungle jabbed and swatted to enter the interior.

"Don't be disappointed," she said. "There will be time for us."

"I'm sorry, Elena. You just have no idea how much I…" He jerked the Jeep to the left. "—care for you. I've wanted you from the very beginning. I waited and wondered if you'd ever be able to trust. I'd given up hope on your wanting to open your heart and your body to someone, but I was okay with it. What was most important was that you learned to feel safe again."

She sighed, unable to speak after his confession. She'd not known men like Brady Scott existed. She'd grown up under her father's strict rule, him more concerned about what was happening in his lab than with his own family. Her community had been dominated by women, because from the time boys reached manhood, they were enticed to join the cartel.

She squeezed his hand, hoping it was enough to convey her feelings.

"Okay, they're stopping up ahead. Time to focus on the

mission."

He watched her mark their location on her running GPS app. She was up to something with that mapping device. He just had to figure out what it was before she put herself or someone else in danger.

Chapter Nine

The view from their balcony was breathtaking. Colored lights from beneath crystal blue swimming pool water illuminated a white, sandy oasis. Fire bowls lit the night as lovers, like moths, were drawn to the warmth of their glow. The evening had turned cool as light winds wisped off the gentle waves twelve stories below.

Elena was lost in the moment. Her mind screamed with dread for Marguerite and desire for Brady. There was only one of those two things she could do anything about at the moment, but it was too soon. She'd dropped her guard and Brady was there to move into her safe space.

She wanted him, but she knew her mind was too clouded by the other issues to allow her to concentrate fully on being intimate. Elena also struggled with the reality that she probably wouldn't survive this negotiation for her niece and data exchange. She was okay with that as long as her only blood relative would survive. Should she enjoy what might be her last night? Brady would be the perfect celebration of life and the love she had grown to know for him.

"What's on your mind, Elena?" Brady asked as he joined her on the balcony.

White wicker chairs dotted a space around a matching glass coffee table. Soft lights lined the railing to create just enough atmosphere for romance, but not enough for sharing secret plans for defeating the cartel. He poured another flute full of champagne and handed it to her.

"Brady, are you trying to get me drunk?" She leaned out, over the railing.

"No, that's not the way I operate." He nudged closer to her.

"Oh, so you operate, huh? How's this operation going so far?"

"Well, since I don't consider my feelings for you a tactical plan, I assume you're referring to the cartel." He tipped back a sip of champagne.

"Really? And what exactly are your feelings for me?" She groaned a bit. Her own forwardness caught her off guard a little.

"I'm here, aren't I? I've always been here for you. I want to protect you and support you to be completely happy and safe." His right hand slid across the top of her left one.

Elena felt the warmth inside her body rise to a boil. Brady's words were setting her soul ablaze. She knew it wasn't idle chatter between opposite sexes in a shared hotel room. He had always been there. Even when everyone else became occupied with their own lives and operations, Brady always remained.

"Is it wrong?" she whispered.

"What?"

"That we're standing up here looking out over this gorgeous night and talking about our feelings, while we know what tomorrow holds?" She nuzzled into a hug. "My heart has never been heavier nor happier than right now, but I feel the guilt of Marguerite's terror."

Brady's muscular arm pulled her tighter. He pressed his face against the top of her head and she rode the rise and fall of his thick, defined chest. There was nothing more to say. She knew he understood. It was what allowed her to feel for him and let him touch her without threat or fear. She wanted to give herself to him fully.

"I tell you what, we've got a long day tomorrow. How about we just turn in and give our minds and emotions a break?" he suggested.

Reluctantly, she agreed.

"Brady, I appreciate you more than I may ever be able to tell you. I may not survive this ordeal, but please promise me you'll get Marguerite to safety."

Brady scowled. "Why wouldn't you survive this?"

She bit on the inside of her cheek. He wasn't stupid—she had to measure every word.

"I meant just in case."

"There'll be no just in case. You're with three of the best operatives in the world. We will protect you, but you've got to promise to do what we tell you. Deal?" He glared into her eyes. It felt like he was examining her soul.

Elena turned away. "Deal."

She squeezed her cell phone while shuffling to the bathroom. It continued to buzz, but she needed the time to think through her options. She cared about Brady. Trusted him. Archer and Audrey, she felt, were there out of obligation to Brady. And while she admired the sacrifice they were willing to make, she couldn't allow the three of them to be harmed.

Locking the door behind her, she twisted the shower knob to high and clicked on the in-mirror television. She pressed herself as far from the bathroom door as possible before opening her phone's screen.

Time is up

I've got it. It's coming, she replied.

Bring it now or you'll be recovering her corpse instead of rescuing her

Hurt her and no data

Tsk, tsk, puta. Hurt is such a strong word. And she feels so good. Just like you did. Such soft skin you both have.

Elena's chest tightened and she struggled for her next breath. Memories of the nonstop assaults over several days caused her gut to clench into a tightened knot. The thoughts of wanting, begging, praying to die sent bile up and into her mouth.

Do not touch her

Fury guided her fingers as they pumped with the need to hurt someone.

Say please

"Fuck off," snarled Elena.

Don't touch her. Last warning.

Say please

You touch her and I toss all the data

She typed while sliding her hand across her forehead. The steam from the shower had created a sauna effect in the bathroom.

I wonder if she'll scream like you did when we brand her.

Elena went lightheaded at the thought, remembering the searing pain. A sob escaped.

I'm bringing the data, she repeated. *Don't touch her.*

Elena slid the rest of the way onto the ceramic tile bathroom floor. Her cries were captured and concealed by the noise, but Brady would soon suspect more than a shower was going on. Time was becoming critical. It was up to her—it was her family, after all.

* * * *

"Declan, I think your situation is much more serious right now. We're going to run a swap and grab. Crap, you're still stuck in Somalia."

Brady ran his fingers through his hair. He paced along the

balcony while taking a glance back inside for Elena.

"Brady, this has to be one of the dumbest things you've ever done. How the hell can you think it's okay? Do you not realize what the cartel has done to our family?"

The scenario at hand was surreal. Brady, a highly trained SEAL, was in a foreign country on a horribly fake passport trying to battle the cartel, while Declan, who was in another foreign country without operational credentials, was trying to save nine warriors chased by deadly indigenous rebels. Had it been any other two men, the reality would be lost to fantasy or imagination.

"Maybe so, but it was either we go with her or she was coming alone."

"We?" Declan shouted.

Brady pinched his unbuttoned cotton shirt with his thumb and middle finger to fan himself. Sweat appeared—nervous sweat.

"Uh, yeah. I asked Audrey and Archer to come along." Brady collapsed into a wicker chair. "Come on, Dec. You know we couldn't let her go alone. After all she's done for us, and we weren't there for her. What choice did she have? What choice did I have?"

"I'm on my way there." Declan's tone shifted.

"No need, bro. Alpha Team is priority." Brady stood back up and leaned over the balcony.

"The nine men were never in jeopardy. Elena actually did save their asses, and they made it back to an exfil site where a bug-out chopper hauled them off to the embassy."

Brady took a relieved breath and stepped back into the lavish suite to tell Elena the good news, but he stopped short. He thought he heard water running and he swore he heard crying. He hated that she was dealing with so many emotions, but he knew she'd rather do so privately. So he gave her the space she needed and focused on Declan's concern.

"I'm sorry I put everyone in a fix."

"Brady, don't be sorry. You did the right thing. I guess in hindsight I did jump down her throat. All I was worried about at the time were the men and the contract. I should've trusted her judgment."

"No problem. We'll work all of this out."

"I feel like I failed her," Declan said.

Brady could hear the regret in his friend's voice. He knew how caring Declan was, and also how committed he was to the people who worked for him. "Declan, you've shown your appreciation in more ways than words. She knows how you feel."

"Thanks."

"No problem. Let's move forward."

"Shane and I will be there in less than a day."

"Dude, that's a twenty-one-hour flight."

"If you're on commercial. Like I said, Shane and I are on our way. Can y'all hold tight?"

Brady's chest tightened. He knew the truth—Elena's patience had run out.

"I don't think we've got that luxury."

"I understand. We're coming anyway. Do the best you can to minimize the damage."

"I'm trying, but they hold a big card over our heads."

"I can't imagine what Elena or her niece are going through. Have you tried negotiating directly with the cartel?"

"No. She's managed the comms via the encrypted texts." A fact that they still had to address.

"See if you can plug yourself into the process. My money is your money. Spare no expense."

"Thanks, Declan, but you know it's the data they want. Theirs and ours."

"I see, but between us only. That is nonnegotiable."

Brady dropped his eyes. "Understood."

Brady ended the call. He gulped a swig from what was left of his champagne. He needed to take stock of what was happening. Was he too close? In less than forty-eight hours, he'd accompanied his heart's crush to Mexico like a love-sick puppy to fight one of the deadliest cartels on the planet. Not only that, but he'd commandeered a MacKenzie Security jet, the pilot, and two employees. And, with no real plan, he'd kept it all a secret from one of the best men he knew.

He kicked his feet onto the railing and drew another gulp. The warm winds brushed against his face, but his mind raced over his conversation with Declan.

"We gotta pull back and think this through," he whispered.

"Pull what back?" Elena challenged him.

His feet flopped to the floor, and his momentum knocked the champagne bottle over without breaking. He watched the liquid pour out instead of facing her.

"Tell me, Brady. What are you planning now?"

Elena faced him, fists at her hips. He tried to reach out for her but she kicked at the bottle and walked back inside the suite. He had to handle this the right way—objectively.

"Elena, can we discuss this without the emotion?" He held his hands up.

"Without emotions? Are you serious? That's my family you're talking about."

Brady bit at the inside of his cheek because he knew it was all a mistake. There'd be no controlling Elena during the mission. Her emotions were understandably connected, and in hindsight, he shouldn't have allowed her to maintain the cell phone messaging. His heart hurt for her. He wanted to rush into that guarded compound and murder every one of those bastards, but he knew better.

"Elena, you're in over your head. I'm begging you to let us handle this. It's what we do. We will get her back safe. I swear on my life."

"You just said you wanted to pull back. What does that mean? Go back to Surrender and wait it out?" she asked, on the verge of hysteria.

"Look at yourself," he barked.

It was his command voice, usually reserved for undisciplined recruits and cocky criminals. But she needed to get a grip—and fast. Stunned, she stopped.

"Open up. Y'all okay in there?" Archer banged on the adjoining interior door.

Brady eased the door open. "Yeah, it's okay. Just going over a few details for tomorrow."

"She can't handle it," Audrey said, assessing Elena as if she were something smudged on a slide under a microscope. "She'll do something stupid and get us all killed. But, what the hell. Here I am making sacrifices for my friends instead of taking vacation time with my husband. Maybe we'll get to spend some time together in the same body bag."

"Audrey," Archer said. "Everyone's tempers are high. Let's sleep it off."

Elena watched her arm cock back and throw the crystal champagne flute against the wall, almost like an out-of-body experience. She regretted it as soon as she did it. She was only trying to save her niece. It wasn't her plan to get anyone killed, and if they'd all listened and stayed home, it wouldn't even be a possibility.

"That's enough," Brady said. "Audrey is right. Your emotions are going to get us all killed. You're done with this. You'll hand over the encrypted cell and let the rest of us handle the mission."

"I'd like to see you try," she whispered.

"You honestly think you're in any position to take on the cartel?"

"Then go home, Brady. Just go home." She started back toward the bathroom.

"Okay, I will. But ask yourself how you'd handle this. You've managed high-stakes ops for years now. If your team was in this fix, what would you do? Didn't you just report that Titus's unwillingness to listen was what caused his fall? How is what you're doing any different?"

Elena looked as if she'd been slapped. She didn't say a word, but instead, turned on her heel and walked into the second bedroom of their suite, shutting the door behind her. Brady heard the click of the lock and knew it was no use to pursue her.

Maybe the morning would bring clarity for them both.

Brady changed into a pair of old gym shorts and pulled off his T-shirt. While he brushed his teeth, he saw his cell phone buzzing. It was a message from Archer. Elena was officially off the mission, and he, Audrey, and Brady would meet at 0700 for breakfast to decide a workable plan.

Chapter Ten

Zero three hundred hours.

"Here goes nothing."

Elena was careful to slip through the luxury suite. It was only three in the morning. She brushed her hands over her wrinkled clothes. Trying to save time and remain quiet, she'd slept in the clothes she would wear to venture out. She also figured brushing her teeth would really be less than a wise use of time, and knew that Brady would awake at the slightest noise.

She tiptoed through the living area. The door to Brady's bedroom was still closed. It was a quick step into the common foyer and to the elevator. She felt a snake of excitement up her spine and dread that weighed like lead in the pit of her stomach. She watched the lights blink and the elevator click off floors as it climbed to the twelfth.

Elena hopped over the threshold and her finger quivered as she jabbed it toward the lobby button. Although it only took a few seconds for the double doors to slide securely closed, she held her breath. She wouldn't have been surprised had Brady or one of the other two appeared in the door to stop her.

She collapsed against the far wall and exhaled as the doors

slid shut and she felt the slight disjoin between her feet and the elevator floor as it rapidly descended. Her knees flexed as the metal box stopped and the doors jiggled without opening. Suddenly, she clutched her chest. What if Brady had taken the stairs and was waiting for her? She held her breath as the same doors that had provided her escape now offered potential betrayal.

The coast was clear.

Elena cat-walked through the vast and luxurious lobby, waving awkwardly at the attendant on the main door. He immediately struck her as peculiar. About five feet and five inches, he seemed to carry himself much taller. Sinister instead of swarthy, his glare tempted her to find another exit. Instead, she persisted.

"Good morning, ma'am. Early start?" the man asked.

"Good morning. I like to take an early morning walk." She nipped at her fingernail.

"But it's a quarter after three." His face sported a curious expression.

She crossed both arms tight to her chest. "I guess I still have jet lag. Not used to the time change." She chuckled.

"True. Be careful, and please remain on the property." He spoke in a slight whistle.

"I'll try."

"Try hard, ma'am. We cannot guarantee your safety once you leave the property."

"I'll keep that in mind." Elena rushed out through the revolving door.

She sensed his eyes were still glued to her. It caused her skin to pimple in goose bumps. She wanted to look back, but her body turned rigid with a sudden fear of being alone. She bent down to pretend to tie her shoe and peeked beneath her elbow. He was gone.

Elena fired up her phone's run tracker app and waited for yesterday evening's route to upload. It was almost five miles, but she knew that as the crow flew, it was much shorter. She decided to give the most direct route a try.

Next, she checked her Cryptocat app to see that the cartel had sent yet another message. It was a continuing escalation of threats. She knew they were close to running out of patience. While they wanted the data from the MacKenzie Security's RMS, they were also volatile enough to cut off their own nose to spite their face without giving it a second thought.

Elena's steps fell heavy and uncertain as she traversed the immaculately manicured resort complex. She greeted staff along the way toward the outer edges. Each face was examined to ensure there wasn't a repeat of the door attendant. He still creeped her out. What if he worked for the cartel?

Elena arrived at a braided rope with a sign in both English and Spanish warning guests not to leave the protected property. She looked back and wondered if she should wait for the other three. A hard exhale and she steeled her thoughts to move forward. Their hesitations might jeopardize Marguerite's life. She'd not be a party to that hesitation.

Her sense of vulnerability was incredible the second her left foot touched down on the other side of the rope. It was as though an entirely dark world had just shifted against her. She also noticed another sign on the opposite side. It pleaded with guests to return to the property. That warning was obviously for people who didn't have lives to save.

Her first two unexpected challenges were the density of the jungle's brush and the complete absence of light. Of course the only light she had was the cell phone's flashlight. She hesitated to use that because it would soon drain her battery.

Elena began to pull and thrash through the thick matrix of vines and foliage. She tried her best to move quietly, but in the brief moments of silence she was reminded of the abundant reptilian existence. She decided she'd just not think about their slithery, cold presence and make her way toward the other side.

Zero three forty hours.

Elena hadn't gone a quarter mile before she felt herself tumbling down a steep and unstable bank, directly into a ravine. Her head was jerked up and back by what felt like a low-hanging vine. Sharp palm fronds sliced into her skin like razors and both feet were rendered useless by the thicket of roots and foliage underfoot. Elena groaned as she continued to fall but she refused to scream.

She landed in a watery pitch. It felt and smelled like a muck of mud and stagnant watershed drainage. Her left ankle burned but she was even deeper below the canopy and it was darker still. She'd dropped her cell phone during the tumble. Elena felt the first tear begin to well up in the corner of her eye. No freaking way—she jammed her muddied palm against her cheek—too much to do for tears.

She was in a jam.

Elena sat and tried to calmly assess herself for injuries other than her left ankle. Sure, she felt the stings of cuts to her skin. The vine that clutched her throat had left a singed brush burn, as best she could tell. She felt the dripping wetness from what had to be her blonde wig that had jostled crooked over her skull. She grabbed a handful of the fake hair and tore it off.

She was soaking wet and caked in what she thought was mud. She gingerly pressed her left foot against what ground she could find that didn't absorb her shoe with the slightest of pressure. It seemed like she'd be able to move on it, but it was going to hurt like hell.

It was darker than closing her eyes. Elena craned her neck to look at what she assumed was up, but there were no indicators of which way led to back out. It was still hours from daylight, and even on the sunniest of days, the thick covering of jungle shielded the ground from the light.

"Time to think like Brady," she whispered. "What would he do?"

Suddenly the frigid scales of something disgusting crawled across her right hand where it supported her body.

"Screw this," she squeaked out and shook her hand furiously.

Elena made a best guess and began to claw her way out. It did no good to stand. The slope's grade was too steep to move up, but at least she knew it meant elevation. Her hands slapped against sloppy muck, while the weight of her torso caused each knee strike to submerge her thighs deeper into the abyss.

Red hot pricks across each forearm paralyzed her. She knew instantly that she'd maneuvered through an ant pile. Painful at best, deadly at worst, if covered by them. She kept moving and instead of swiping at what couldn't be seen, she smashed the fiery feelings in her forearms into the coolness of the murky earth.

"Damn ants," she murmured.

At least she'd hoped they were ants and not the indigenous spiders or, even worse, scorpions. Staying still wouldn't answer her question, nor would it help ease her pain. She continued to plow her way up the incline.

"No way," she laughed.

Up about another ten feet was the soft glow of what she knew to be her cell phone. Either that or it was one giant, rectangular-shaped firefly. It encouraged her to know she was moving along the right path. She coddled it like an old friend and fought the temptation to shine its light on her wounds.

Elena knew her time was running out. Once Brady discovered she was gone, he'd hightail it to the golf cart. For all she knew, he could've already been there. She kept her head low and trudged through the same wiry matrix of natural obstructions that plummeted her in the first place. From the time on her phone's screen to the time she crested onto a trail, it was about another twenty minutes.

Zero four thirty hours.

Elena swatted at her clothes but she only felt the boggy saturation. The morning sun would soon take care of that, and she dreaded the baked feeling. Then she huffed while standing on the trailhead because she realized how much time had been wasted. And if she was honest with herself, she was completely lost. The run tracker app only presented the route she'd taken yesterday. It didn't give reroute directions like a car's GPS navigation system.

She was, however, able to see the beacon of lights that radiated from the resort. She'd follow that back to the ropes and start over. It would take her another twenty minutes to backtrack to the point of initial entrance. She felt the press of time lost and that Brady would soon be up and on his way to intervene. Elena limped on her injured ankle. She knew enough to stay close to the edge just in case she detected a threat.

She ducked into the bushes as she saw something breaking the variances between light and dark. It was a person. She glared into the void. Whoever it was seemed to be walking around just on the outside of the resort's security barrier. Was it that same creepster from inside the lobby? It sure wasn't Brady. Although she couldn't identify who it was, this person was maybe five feet and six or seven inches. Brady's six-foot-two-inch frame would've dwarfed this shadowy figure.

Once the coast was finally clear, she ambled closer to what would have to become her new starting point toward the golf carts. An avid jogger, Elena knew that on a good day she could average an eight-minute mile. This wasn't a good day. She'd be lucky to walk the five miles in under two hours.

She set her watch. It was already zero five hundred hours.

"Dammit," she muttered. If her calculations were correct, she'd make it to the golf cart around zero seven hundred. Brady would be up by then.

* * * *

Zero six forty-five hours.

Elena was almost spot-on with her calculations for finding the golf carts. She'd gutted it out to come in under the two hours. It was a much tougher run than any marathon or triathlon she'd ever completed. She felt the swelling erupting over her hiking boot. Soaked from the morning's dew and her sweat, shivers of cold attacked her as cool wind blew over her skin. She rummaged through the supplies to find a blanket and patted herself off.

Elena hopped in the golf cart closest to the path and finally took a breather. It was short-lived as worry set in. Her worry gave way to fear and eventually thoughts of failure. There were no keys in the ignition. What could she have been thinking? Why would there be keys just sitting there?

Her first thought was to call Brady and ask him where the keys could be found. Then she realized the absurdity of even imagining he'd help her.

She looked east to see the jagged fingers of pink and orange rake through a dark onyx sky. Sunup was close. She was not. Elena circled the golf cart and began to frantically run her hands over and below the carriage of the vehicle. She'd seen enough movies to know that hiding keys was usually the best way of protecting them. Besides, what choice did she have?

She looked at the motor with a curious glower.

"Maybe I could hotwire it," she said, but then laughed in

despair—she had no clue how to do that.

She fell to her bruised knees and ran her hands below the rhino-coated bottom like she was caressing a newborn.

"Got it." She waggled the keys above her head.

Elena sent a message to the cartel once she got into the roadway. She wanted to keep them calm until she got close to their location. She maneuvered onto the highway, Mexico 307, and set her focus on the seven-hour drive to Calakmul. The tiny town would give her a place to set up shop while still being far enough away from the cartel's fortified base inside the commandeered Mayan temple.

Without issue, she figured to arrive around two. Afternoons in July would really stink, but not making it at all would stink worse. She plugged her cell into the golf cart's direct battery recharger, thankful that she'd be able to communicate with the cartel when needed.

There were no cars on the highway, except that she had noticed a set of headlights when she first pulled onto the highway while it was still dark. There wasn't much in the way of anything along 307. It was only a means of getting from abject poverty in the country to extreme wealth at the beachside resorts.

Her cell phone powered up and immediately the ringing mixed into winds that bustled across the open-topped vehicle. It was Brady. She let it go to voicemail and stuffed the phone beneath her thigh. There was already a small pool of moisture on the seat as the earliest of the morning sun was raging its vehemence against the earth. The phone continued to ring.

Zero seven twenty hours.

She shaded her eyes from the glare that bounced around the interior. In her haste, she'd also forgotten sunshades and a hat.

She bit at her lip and thought maybe she should've given this entire scenario the consideration Brady suggested.

Where the hell are you Brady texted.

Going to get my niece

You are going to die. Stop where you are and wait for me

No

How will you get through the highway checkpoints? You left your passport in the room. I'm begging you to stop where you are. I will meet you.

"Dammit," she said, beating the steering wheel with her palms.

Screams hitched in her chest as she wheeled the vehicle onto the highway's shoulder and stopped. It continued to add up to an impossible situation. She had no clue how to avoid the checkpoints, much less where they were. She remembered when she lived on the peninsula that the corrupt *federales* would intensify the number and location of roadblocks as she drew closer to the cartel's home base.

Her throat was sticky. She grabbed for a bottle of water in the console. It was empty. She'd also forgotten to carry water. She tossed the plastic container in the back of the golf cart and twisted to look for a jug.

"Surely Audrey thought to pack for hydration," she hoped.

Her eyes blinked back the sweat from the encrusted lids that weighed heavily from the morning's exertion. She sat up rigid and then crumpled behind the foam-padded seat. Was that the same vehicle she'd spotted earlier? She began to wonder why it hadn't overtaken her since she'd started her trek. She kept purposefully below the speed limit to avoid police detection, so any legitimate motorist would've gained on her by that point. Her heart pounded at the thought of being followed.

She fumbled for her phone and hit redial.

"Brady?" She began.

"Elena, what are you doing? This is suicide."

She peered into her rearview mirror. There was indeed a vehicle in the distance. It seemed to have been there since she had first taken off from the grove of trees. Now she was certain.

"Brady, I think they're following me." She owed him an explanation, but there wasn't time.

"Elena. Do not let them stop you. Drive over them if you have to." His voice ticked up in emphasis.

"They won't stop me and neither will you. I'm going to do what is right. I don't care if it costs me my life."

"Listen to what you're saying," he pleaded. "Dying will do no one any good. If death is your goal, then save everyone the effort and drive that golf cart off a cliff. Otherwise, listen to me."

"What if they're following me?"

"Focus, Elena. You're driving into the shark's mouth. They won't stop you. They're just making sure you continue moving forward. Like corralling a lost calf. Please understand what I'm telling you. They'll stay back and wait until you get to a checkpoint. Then the guards will quietly remove you and no one will ever know you existed."

"Why?" Panic started to eat at her.

"It's too messy trying to stop a moving car. What if you crashed or lost the flash drive? Just keep driving slow and they'll stay back."

"Drive? I'm parked on the shoulder." Her eyes frantically scanned every direction with an anticipation of doom.

"No, don't park," he ordered. "You've got to get moving. Preferably away from the cartel headquarters."

"What about Marguerite?" Her heart was pounding so fast the thump was almost painful in her chest.

"Don't take this the wrong way, but Marguerite is not the issue right now."

"The hell she isn't," Elena said.

"Woman, I love you, but I need you to understand this right

now. Get back on the highway and drive. If they capture you, Marguerite is dead. Do you understand me?"

She started to reply, but then realized what he'd said. "You're picking now of all times to tell me you love me?"

* * * *

Brady knew his timing was wrong, but his feelings were right. If she was on a suicide mission, he needed to give her something to live for. He gathered his thoughts, willing her to stay strong, but before he could utter a word, he heard a crash and the whoosh of Elena's breath.

Screams and angry voices filled the phone.

And the line went dead.

Chapter Eleven

"Declan, we've got problems," Brady said into the satellite phone.

"We're in the air. What's the issue?"

Brady pointed directions for Archer, who steered the second golf cart like a ten-year-old at the bumper car park.

"Elena decided to go solo and bugged out before we realized she was gone. I had her on the phone, but it sounded like she was taken by force."

"Shit," Declan said. "Do you know where she went down?"

"No, but she was on her cell phone. We should be able to grab a triangulation on her last signal ping. At least we'll know a mile marker." Brady pulled up the contact information for Willa at HQ.

"We'll be there around seventeen hundred hours," Declan said. "We'll chopper to wherever you are. I'm calling all hands on deck for this one. Brady, you're at the tip of this spear. Make sure you go deadly, but cover your tracks as long as possible. Once the cartel places that region on red alert, we won't be able to take a piss without getting our dicks shot off."

"Roger that. See you soon." Brady clung to the suicide bar as

Archer veered off the highway to avoid a truck full of livestock.

"You should have handcuffed her," Audrey said.

Brady yelled over the wind. "Maybe under better circumstances. Can you rally Mossad resources in the area?"

"I'm afraid not. Most are locals sympathetic to the Israeli people's plight. Getting the golf carts and arsenal was a task. I wouldn't count on any of them to even know how to fire the weapons they provided."

"Gotcha," Brady said.

"Any idea how far along this road she was?" Archer asked.

"No clue." The phone was still ringing for HQ, and he let out a sigh of relief when Willa answered. He'd lost track of the time back home.

"Willa?"

"Well, well. If it isn't Lieutenant Hottie. I was expecting your call. Declan sent the order for an all-call alert. I've activated Darcy and Brant."

Brady sighed and shook his head at the nickname. At least she didn't call him that in front of his men. He hoped. Willa was unpredictable. But to correct her was futile. She was a perpetual ray of sunshine, which was a nice change of pace considering the seriousness of their jobs, and all she had to do was bat those baby blues and let her dimple flash, and everyone—men and women alike—would fall all over themselves to help her out. She had a gift.

"How did you get in contact with my brother so fast?" he asked.

"He and Darcy flew in a couple of days ago so he could handle a board meeting while Declan is out of country," she said. "I saw him standing in the cafeteria waiting on food and I said, 'Hey, Brant, your brother needs you.' It really wasn't that hard to get him on board. Apparently, he feels some kind of loyalty to you. Unlike my evil twin Martie, who has made it her life habit of sleeping with every man I've ever had an interest in."

Brady rolled his eyes and couldn't help but smile. "Focus," he said. "Who else?"

"The Devlins checked in and confirmed the assignment. They're chartering a flight out of Reagan as we speak."

"Perfect," he said. "The Devlins were with us when we dealt with the cartel the first time. They're familiar with their habits and the area."

"I'm still waiting on Cade to respond. He's been tied up at the Dallas office, but I should hear from him at any time."

"Great job, Willa."

"Anything for you, sugar. You can pay me back by setting me up with that long, tall drink of water you came in with. I think his name is Mick."

"He's also married with three kids," Brady said. "And I keep telling you, I'm not running a SEAL matchmaking service."

"I don't see why not," she said, her sigh audible. "You're missing out on a hell of a financial opportunity. Women would pay big bucks for that kind of access."

His lips twitched. "I'll bring it up at the next board meeting."

"That's all I ask. What else do you need from me?"

"I need a location on Elena's cell. We were talking when it went dead. It sounded like it was hung up instead of the battery dying or destroyed. See if you can…"

"I'm on it. I'll get you a last ping location and an active track of her phone if it's still transmitting."

"What are you? A mind reader?" Brady asked.

"I'm a millennial, Lieutenant Hottie. We rock technology."

"Let me know as soon as you get anything," he said.

"Will do. Anything else?" she asked.

"Yeah. Stop calling me Lieutenant Hottie."

"Is Lieutenant Hot Buns better?"

He sighed, knowing he'd probably asked for that one. "No,

definitely not."

"Bummer. I liked the sound of it," she said. "HQ over and out." And then she disconnected.

Brady looked at Archer. "That Willa is something else."

"Of course she is. She's my niece." Archer's lips twitched. "Audrey and I are really proud of her for turning her life around. She was headed on a path of destruction—alcohol and drugs—and then she got pregnant. She and my daughter are only a couple years apart. Declan took a hell of a chance bringing her on when we asked him to, but she's got a brilliant mind. We just needed to get her out of the environment she was in and show her she had other choices for her and her son."

"She's a hell of an asset to the team," Brady said. "We're all proud of her. Speaking of," he said as his phone beeped. "We've got incoming." And then his phone buzzed and he saw it was Willa.

"What's up?" he said.

"I just sent Elena's location to your phone. Did it come through?"

He lowered the device and quickly studied the map. "Got it. It looks like we're about five miles out if we stay on this road."

"It's an estimate," Willa said. "I grabbed a ping from her cell during the last call to you, but that ended once the call did. Fortunately, but stupidly, she has a run tracking app on her phone. I keep telling her there are safer ways to keep track of jogging because it's on an open platform. That means she can share her runs real time or post runs, but even if she sets the app to private, the device continues tracking her through the phone. It's information anyone with average technology skills could figure out."

"Why does it keep tracking?"

"Just in case she finishes her run and decides to post it later," she said. "Nothing is truly private. I told her, Brady, but you know how stubborn she can be."

"Well, let's be thankful for her stubbornness this time around. Where is she?"

"Actually, she's moving at a steady pace. I overlaid her route onto a topical map based on her latitude and longitude coordinates. Best I can tell is she's about a half mile off of the highway and heading uphill."

"Is there a road or trail?"

"Doesn't look like it. Appears to be on foot."

"Thanks. Keep me posted."

Archer slowed the cart. "Look," he said, pointing. "The gravel on that shoulder has fresh tracks. Someone pulled over there not long ago."

"Elena?"

"No," Audrey answered. "Tires don't match. It's a car of some kind. Probably small. The impression isn't deep, as if it were a truck or bigger car, and moisture from the morning's dew is still settled around it. It's very fresh."

"Willa said we're less than five miles from Elena and moving closer. She's tracking her, and it looks like she's on foot, moving up the mountain."

Archer narrowed his eyes at Brady. "How does she know our location to compare distances?"

"I'll tell you later," he said. "But for now, I wouldn't go anyplace you don't want your niece to know about."

"Ha! Told you so," Audrey said from the rear seat.

"Willa and I are going to have a serious talk when we get home," Archer said with a sigh.

"Hold on." Brady grabbed Archer's arm. "Look up there."

Elena's cart was pulled off to the side of the highway's shoulder. A small gray sedan was parked beside it.

"Stop here. Let's take a cover line in those trees and go on foot." Brady pointed as he swung both feet out of the slowing golf cart. "Archer, make sure to bring your phone."

"Why?" he asked while strapping his compact submachine gun across his torso.

"So Willa can direct us to Elena's position. Why else?" Brady smiled.

Audrey hopped from the rear of the golf cart. She too was strapped with a similar rifle and a giant smirk. "See, I told you so."

"Yeah, yeah," he said. "Don't get used to saying that."

"I don't get to say it very often," she said. "I'm going to milk it while I can."

Brady activated the hands-free Bluetooth earpiece and connected with Willa.

"We're on foot. Have both cars in sight but no people. Direct us to her."

"Roger that," Willa said. "She appears to be headed to the summit. From the topographical comparison, it looks like she's about two thousand feet in elevation."

"From where we are, guide us at a ninety-degree angle to intercept her."

"10-4, Lieutenant Hottie." Then she sighed audibly. "Blah, blah, blah. I know, I know. Stop calling you that."

"Hold up, Brady," Audrey said from her rear guard position. "Look between the two cars."

Brady squatted into the brush for concealment as he squinted for a clear view. It was a body. And it didn't look like he'd be getting up again.

"Damn, that wasn't what I was expecting," Brady said.

"Could be a trap. We'll go on your orders. Do you want to move closer?" Archer asked.

Brady scanned the thick overgrowth and listened closely for sounds of feet trampling through the jungle or screams of struggle. It was quiet.

"Negative," Brady said. "You can see where the bullet

opened his head right up."

"You think Elena's armed?" Audrey asked, surprised.

"She can shoot as well as anyone," Brady said. "Did you check the arsenal? Was there anything missing?"

Audrey shrugged. "No idea."

"Then there are two possibilities. She's either armed and was able to take one of them out, or she has someone else trying to help her."

"Or a third scenario," Audrey said. "His own men could've killed him and they're setting us up for a trap."

"That thought did cross my mind," Archer said.

"Either way, there's one less bad guy to deal with."

Brady thought about what Declan had said about covering their tracks. He knew they had to hide the corpse, but it would also put them out in the open.

"Guys, split up into opposing fields of fire and cover me. I've got to drag that body into the woods. Word gets out too soon and we don't stand a fighting chance."

"10-4, Lieutenant Hottie," Audrey said.

Archer snickered and Brady narrowed his eyes at her, but she just grinned at him. "What? I heard it through the Bluetooth while you were talking with Willa. I think it's cute."

"Not a word to anyone," he said.

"Oh no," she said, her grin widening. "I'd never do that."

Brady rolled his eyes, figuring he was going to catch hell for the nickname later. He was quick to traverse the tree line. It wouldn't protect him from bullets, but it helped hide him from immediate threats. He crouched about twenty yards from the rear bumper of the small sedan and looked back to Archer, waiting for the all clear.

Archer gave the signal.

A quick sprint across an open area landed Brady nearly on top of the dead man. He was dark complected, his stature small.

His face was gone. The bullet had been fired point blank. He was dressed similarly to the staff at the resort. Even his nametag showed he worked there.

Brady made his way back to Archer and Audrey.

"He looks like a local from the resort. I'm betting whoever else is chasing her isn't trained—they're just desperate."

"Desperation usually leads to death," Audrey said.

"Ahh, there's my bride. You're such a romantic," Archer said, chuckling.

Brady half-smiled as he headed into the brush with the smaller man's body. He'd missed teaming up with the MacKenzie agents. There was a closeness and camaraderie similar to his SEAL team. Being able to joke during times of crisis was a good thing. Soldiers who became too stone-faced at the onset of conflict often ended up with tragic results.

"You're in their direct travel line, Lieutenant Hottie," Willa said in his earpiece. He'd been so focused on the body, he'd forgotten they were connected.

"You're going to be our eyes," he told her. "Guide us through. We're in a triangular fire team formation. I'm on point."

"Roger," she said. "Looks like you're going to swing right and head close to twenty yards. You'll see a slight clearing."

He moved quietly in the direction suggested, Archer and Audrey flanking his sides. They maintained their distance from each other so in the event they began taking on fire, they wouldn't all get hit. Their separation also allowed them to shoot freely without getting in front of each other's lines of fire.

"Found the clearing," Brady whispered.

He saw a creek bed with a shallow amount of green water flowing downstream, and he immediately moved them into the middle of it. It wasn't the best route to conceal their approach, but it was the quickest.

"She's not moved in a while," Willa said.

"Perfect, it gives us a chance to make up ground," Brady said.

"Willa, can you text Elena? Maybe she'll reply with intel," Audrey said.

"Been texting her. No reply. I'm guessing it's on silent and her hands are full with being a badass."

Brady grunted and held up a fist that signaled for the others to stop and hold their positions. He tuned his hearing into anything that sounded out of the ordinary. The brush was thick and tore at his clothes, but he maintained focus on listening for unnatural movements.

"Nothing," he said. "Let's move."

"Hold up a second," Willa said. "She's showing a slight turn back to the left. About fifty yards to your west and a quarter mile north. If you move toward the ten o'clock position, I think you'll run smack into her."

"Roger," Brady said. "Adjusting position."

The trio were like ghosts. Brady didn't even hear them, much less anyone else, but he thought there were odd breaks in the shadows up ahead.

"Hold," he said. "We got tangoes."

"Oh, yeah," Audrey said. "I see them."

"I don't see shit," Archer admitted.

"Just hold your position," Audrey said. "I'll move."

Audrey slithered through the jungle like a snake, and Brady admired her ability to move without detection. He locked in on the person hunched in the brush like an awkward panther, waiting to ambush them.

"She's close," Brady whispered to Archer. "Be ready in case she draws a crowd."

"I'm always ready."

Audrey hunted the man with stealth. He never felt her—never moved—never looked back. Audrey didn't waste time. She sprang, her hand forcing his head back, exposing the thick veins in his neck. The KA-BAR was in her hand in a flash, and she sliced it quickly across his neck, easing him gently to the ground. It was almost humane in its speed and lethality—the man never saw it coming.

Audrey returned to the formation, so Brady slid back to point and Archer moved back to left flank. He guided them away from the initial path clearing and into a deeper, darker section of the jungle.

"Twenty yards," Willa whispered.

The anticipation and tension built steadily, and it was obvious even Willa could feel it all the way back in Surrender because he could hear her breathing escalate on the other end of the line.

"I've got a visual," Brady said. "Elena's up ahead, but there are at least two threats to the west of her. Looks like they're climbing ahead and over her position."

"Can you take them out?" Archer asked.

"Not sure," Brady said. "The distance is okay, but I don't have a clear shot."

"Best course?" Audrey asked.

"We'll waste too much time trying to outflank them," Brady said. "Going east only moves us further away."

"Full-on assault?" Archer asked.

"10-4. Straight ahead." Brady recalculated all the possibilities in his mind and determined that full force was still the best option. They had the element of surprise and training on their side.

"Umm..." Willa said through the headset. "I don't mean to rain on your parade, Lieutenant Hottie, but what if Elena shoots at y'all, thinking you're the bad guys? I thought she was armed."

"Are you ever going to call me by my name?" Brady asked with a sigh.

"You have a name?" Willa said, feigning surprise.

"Very funny," Brady said. "But no, I'm not worried about Elena shooting us. Chances are they've already disarmed her. If they haven't, they're the dumbest criminals in the history of the world. Audrey and I will take care of the two tangoes and Archer will secure Elena. In and out. Piece of cake."

"They're closing in," Archer said. "The window of opportunity is here."

"On my count," Brady said. "Three...two...one..."

Audrey fell in line behind him, and they moved swiftly straight toward the targets, their bodies bladed out so they each covered all angles. The tangoes had no clue what was about to hit them. Neither did Elena. And she was a wild card. Hopefully she'd had enough training to remember to assess with her eyes before she made any noise and alerted the enemy.

Brady moved stealthily through the underbrush and overhangs of the trees. He kept a watchful eye on Elena and Archer's progress toward her, but his main focus was on the two armed men up ahead. He felt the clock ticking down in his mind, and he wanted to rush, but patience was the key. Rushing an op was how the good guys ended up dead.

He signaled for Audrey to stop, and they took cover behind a vine-covered tree. Archer was circling back behind Elena, and he wanted to give him plenty of time to get in position. Timing was going to be everything.

Elena stood stiffly, her back straight and her chin jutted with stubborn pride. She was stronger than she gave herself credit for, and it was everything he could do not to rush to her and take her in his arms. He noticed her wrists were bound in front of her, and her clothes were dirty and scuffed from what was probably the altercation when they disarmed her. But for the most part, she looked unharmed. Pissed. But unharmed.

Their window was closing tighter. His gaze went back to the two Hispanic men dressed in jeans and tattered fieldhand shirts guarding her. One had a shotgun, and the other had a machete. The goal was to take them both down without a shot being fired.

The last thing they wanted was to draw more attention to themselves.

He made eye contact with Archer, and Archer gave the nod that he was in position.

"No gunfire," he whispered to Audrey.

She drew her KA-BAR and nodded. And then he held up three fingers so both Audrey and Archer could see them, and counted down the signal to go.

Brady trusted Archer to keep Elena safe, and he and Audrey rushed forward to intercept the two tangoes. Charging toward the one with the shotgun, leaving Audrey with the other, he immediately grabbed his wrist and punched out with his other arm, hitting the man in his elbow. There was a sickening crunch and the shotgun dropped to the ground. Brady slapped his hand over the man's mouth before he could scream and then jerked his head to the side, breaking his neck.

He looked over in time to see Audrey dodge a vicious swipe of the machete, but the man left himself wide open and she kicked him in the balls, bringing him to his knees. She jerked his head back and sliced his throat and then let him fall to the ground.

"Clear," Audrey said. "No sign of others."

Brady was already heading toward Elena. Her gaze never left his, and there was an intensity in the way she looked at him, as if they were connected by an invisible string. Archer released her restraints and as soon as she was free, she ran toward Brady and jumped in his arms.

"I'm so sorry," she said, her words tumbling out. "I should've listened. I was just so scared, and I'm not good at trusting other people."

"No kidding," he said, raising a brow. She felt good in his arms. She was small, petite, but he felt the strength in her muscles. "I keep thinking someday you'll learn."

"Because you love me," she said, repeating his earlier

declaration.

He was going to answer her, but she silenced him when she placed her hands on either side of his cheeks and leaned up to kiss him. It was the first time she'd taken the initiative. The first time that sweet mouth had taken his in a kiss that rocked him to his core. She was tentative, her lips soft and searching, but then she grew bolder and he felt the tip of her tongue trace his lips. Before long they were both panting for breath.

"We should probably take this back to the resort," he said, his lungs heaving. "Things are about to get a little embarrassing the second you move from in front of my body."

"Don't worry, Lieutenant Hottie," Willa said. "Things are already plenty embarrassing. I think I'm going to hang up now."

Chapter Twelve

"There's a checkpoint about two miles ahead," Archer said over the phone a little while later.

They'd trekked back to the golf carts and the sedan that had been left by the side of the road, deciding it was best to split up for the time being.

"Audrey and I will go through first and get a feel for it. We'll signal you once we're clear."

"10-4," Brady said. "We'll hang back."

"What kind of checkpoint? Do you think they're looking for us?"

"We can't know for sure," he said. "Checkpoints are pretty typical. It's a great way to check out who to rob. The best thing we can do is to act like tourists who got too far away from the resort. The cartel gets a kickback from the resort, and when tourism goes down because of crime, they don't get as big of a percentage. The only thing we know for sure is that the four of us are the only people we can trust until the cavalry arrives."

"So, shoot first and ask questions later?" she asked.

"Pretty much," he said. "I'm assuming that's what you did with the body we found back where the cars were parked."

"Nope, not me," she said. "They got in a fight over who

would present me to El Toro. I'm guessing that's the new cartel leader. Apparently, there's a bounty for me and the third guy was making noises about claiming all of it instead of splitting it three ways. So they shot him.

"I know I said it before, but I'm so sorry. I'm not afraid anymore. I've done nothing but put distance between me and everyone who's ever cared about me. Despite telling myself I was strong and that I was better off alone, I was letting the cartel dictate my life, even though I'd put a couple of thousand miles between us. All I can say is thank you for your patience. You don't have to worry about me anymore. I've got faith in the team, and that we'll do whatever we can to save Marguerite."

Brady reached over and squeezed her hand. "Baby," he said, "I've always known you had the strength. From the second I saw you lying in that hospital bed fighting to survive, I knew you had the determination to come through it stronger than ever. I've never lost faith in you."

"I know that," she said softly. "And it makes me love you all the more because of it."

"Hell, you're going to have me sobbing like a baby if you keep that up," he said. But while his eyes were damp, his smile could've lit the world, and he squeezed her hand before letting it go.

"When will the cavalry arrive?" she asked.

"Declan and Shane are still in the air. It's thirteen-thirty hours now, so I expect boots on the ground at the resort in a few hours."

She rolled her eyes. "Y'all drive me crazy. Why can't you just say that it's one-thirty?" Even though she was guilty of the same thing.

He grinned, realizing that she was trying to banter with him. "Because military time is the only time. How are you supposed to know if it's morning or night otherwise?"

Brady's cell rang and he put it on speaker.

"We got through," Archer said. "But give me fifteen minutes, and I'll hop out and circle back on foot so I can cover you. Looks like they're just scoping potential victims. Nothing serious. They did a half-assed search of the car, but I think they were too afraid of Audrey to do much more than that. She growled at one of them."

"Dial it back, Pinocchio," Audrey said. "The only person growling was you when that guy was checking me out."

"Oh, right," Archer said. "Maybe it was me. Now I'm going to have to pull the car over and reclaim my territory. Scratch the fifteen, Brady. Better give me eighteen minutes instead."

Audrey and Elena both laughed at the silly byplay, and Elena felt a lightness to her spirt that she hadn't felt in a long, long time.

"Roger that," Brady said, smiling.

They waited the allotted amount of time before approaching the checkpoint to present their passports. The guards were dressed in oversized uniforms and had machine guns slung over their shoulders. They were young, barely men, and Elena could see how they'd be intimidated by Archer and Audrey.

"Destination?" one of the guards demanded, taking their passports.

"Xpujil," Brady said.

"Reason?"

"We got passes from the resort to see the temples," he said. "We're celebrating our anniversary, so the resort kicked in a few extras for us."

"It was so nice of them," Elena gushed. "We can't wait to tell all our friends to come here. Everyone has been so friendly."

Brady wanted to laugh as the guards fell under Elena's spell. She was a beautiful woman, and all she had to do was bat those long eyelashes and smile and the men were passing them through the checkpoint. Brady all of a sudden understood Archer's need to reclaim his territory.

Brady pulled over after he'd cleared the bend in the highway, and Archer hopped in the back.

"Looking a little flushed, my friend," Brady said, eyeing Archer.

"Give me a little credit, man. I don't do my best work in three minutes, so I gave her a rain check. But it's hot as hell in the direct sun. Audrey is going to meet us at the site."

The drive was smooth as they made their way south, the sun glaring down intensely and beating off the windshield.

"I seriously can't believe these golf carts," Elena said. "They're like golf carts on steroids, and we're going sixty miles an hour without the wind kicking our asses. Who makes these things? I want one."

"Audrey has some Mossad contacts that owed us some favors," Archer said. "These aren't exactly available on the open market. Speaking of Audrey, this is our rendezvous point." He checked his GPS and then scanned the area.

Brady slowed down and caught a movement from the corner of his eye. Before he had time to react, he saw Audrey speeding ahead of him.

Archer grinned. "She'll meet us at the next stop."

Once they turned right onto Mexican Highway 186, the road wasn't as smooth and there was more opportunity for ambush. The terrain changed from desert sun to forests to narrow mountain passes and one-lane dirt roads.

They pulled into what was billed as a resort. It looked like a roach-infested hole in the wall, barely standing on the west side of Xpujil. Brady pulled the golf cart around to the rear of the dilapidated structure. The town was small and condensed into a handful of streets that seemed to crisscross at intersections each block. They didn't see a stoplight, so they doubted electricity was a common convenience.

"This is the tallest building here," Brady explained. "The third floor allows us to see everything. Well, not that there's much to see."

"It's almost sixteen hundred hours, so we're already late. No need rushing into this. Let's get set up and assess the situation. I'm curious whether they know we're in Xpujil or maybe at a closer location. This is still about seventy-five miles out from the Mayan temple."

Archer gathered his gear and gave a small salute as he disappeared behind a nearby building to meet Audrey.

Elena grabbed Brady's arm. She felt her heart swelling with sadness.

"What's wrong?"

"It's becoming too real to be back here. I've been so concerned about Marguerite, I haven't given myself a chance to think how I'd feel seeing it all again."

Brady wrapped his arms around her and held on. She understood the reality that awaited her was much more pressing than the serenity she found in his arms. She'd come to save a life, not fall in love, but as she allowed herself to open up, she realized maybe she came for both.

"You okay to go inside and get situated? I need to make contact with the team and check on their ETA."

"So we're not going to wait?"

"I know the team is coming, but there's no reason we can't start the ball rolling. Agreed?"

She nodded.

Brady grabbed as much gear from the golf cart as he could hoist across his back and shoulders. He motioned for her to go inside—he was on his way inside the lobby too. She knew about the cache of weapons and surveillance equipment. She also knew it would be stolen within seconds of them going inside. She didn't hate her countrymen for stealing. She hated the cartel for imprisoning them into poverty so they were forced to steal.

It took an extra five bucks cash to secure the entire third floor. The place was a large, empty shell. Painted in pinks, yellow, and turquoise, it had been neglected. The pool was a black sludge where iguanas and dogs battled for scraps. Brady led her upstairs and then pushed her behind a crevice when the maintenance man came up behind them to deliver the keys.

"You sure you haven't seen this girl?" the maintenance man asked, holding up a crumpled picture

"Just hand over the key," Brady replied to him in Spanish. "I don't want questions."

The old man's expression shifted. "*No gringo?*"

"No."

Elena braced at the sight of her picture but quickly relaxed when she realized she hadn't been recognized. She assumed the old man had to be blind not to notice her or see that the six-foot-two-inch, blond Thor look-alike was indeed a *gringo*. She pressed her palm against her lips to muffle the chuckle at the conversation the two men were engaged in.

"Here's your key, *mi amigo.*"

"*Gracias.*"

Brady, still lugging all of their gear, grabbed Elena by the elbow and quickly led her back up the stairs. She noticed what looked to have been an elevator, but was now just another trash receptacle.

"What's the deal?"

Brady fumbled with the key but drew his pistol before he shoved the door open with his foot. He entered and quickly cleared the area before allowing Elena to enter.

"Why'd you give him such a hard time?" she asked.

"While I was unloading the car, he told me the cartel had sent out an alert with a picture of you. He asked if I'd seen you and said that there was a thousand dollar bounty on your head."

"Just a thousand?" She planted her fists into her hips, masking her nerves with false bravado.

Brady grinned and rolled his eyes.

"Baby, we can't do anything here. Everyone is desperate for that money, and they'll be turning over random women to the cartel just for the hell of it. We can't trust anyone. Which is why I'm going to tie up and gag our friend and shove him in a closet."

"What should I do?" she asked.

"Put the wig back on."

"Lost it."

He held up the photograph he'd been given by the old man. She still looked the same. He handed her his KA-BAR knife.

"Am I supposed to use this to defend myself?"

"No. Cut your hair off."

* * * *

Brady paced along the balcony. It faced inward, but the mosquito-infested pool didn't serve any purpose. He needed an observation point. At the far end of the third floor balcony, he discovered a service ladder. It was actually a few metal steps welded to a rusted railing. He climbed it but wasn't sure it would support him.

His thumb hit speed dial and he waited for the series of beeps before Willa answered from HQ.

"Can you patch me through to Declan?" he asked.

"Easy as pie," she said. "Hold tight, sugar. They're still in the air."

Brady waited as Willa worked the switchboard.

"MacKenzie," Declan said a few seconds later.

"What's your status?" Brady asked without greeting.

"We're still about a couple of hours out. Anyone else arrive yet?"

Willa, who was patched into the call replied, "No, sir. Cade was the first in country, but last I heard he was held up at customs."

"Those fuckers are more powerful than I imagined. They've sealed off the entire country. Willa, reroute the others into Guatemala. Campeche is less than twenty-five miles from their border."

"And if they get stopped there?"

"Then get everyone a damned parachute," he said.

"Umm…okie dokie," she said. "This job is always interesting. I'll give you that."

"You're a peach, Willa. If anyone can find a way, you can. We've got to get the agents in country before it's too late."

"Roger that, Lieutenant Hottie."

Brady felt a flush of embarrassment at being called that with Declan on the line.

"Willa routed me into the encrypted messaging service. Brady, it's not looking good for the visiting team."

"What do you mean?"

"Rather not in mixed company, but it's getting close to a repeat."

"And?"

"And, I think you four have to roll the dice and make the best play you can. Does she have the flash drive with actual data? If surrendering that is what it takes to save that girl, then the hell with it. Let 'em have it."

"Declan, that's freaking incredible, but she's made a Trojan horse."

"They'll kill her," he barked.

"Well, to be honest, she admitted that when she devised the plan, she didn't expect to come out alive."

"So she knew full well that once her niece was freed into the US, that she'd plant that virus we confiscated into their network?"

"So far, so good."

"And the flash drive is engineered to transmit all of their data to a secured server at Mac Security and the DOJ while destroying their own database?"

"Yes, sir."

"That's fucking brilliant," Declan muttered.

"Except the part about them torturing her to death."

"Yes, of course."

"Willa, can you pull Archer into this call?"

"Will do, Brady."

"He's not with you?"

"No. We took a spot on the west side of the city and they're grabbing a place on the east."

Declan let out a hum that caused Brady's gut to start churning. Brady squatted down behind an H/VAC service shed. He peered across the tiny town and marveled that anyone survived out here. The place was archaic at best. He recalled Elena had originally come from a place not unlike this. It wasn't that he was judging the people. He only knew he'd never make it out here.

"Yo, what's up, Dec?"

"Hey, Archer. You enjoying the vacation?"

"I'm having a ball, but Audrey said she's going to castrate you. We've been to shitty places before, bro, but this has to be at the top."

"I can't imagine, but if Brady was the one who picked it, I know it's gotta suck. Remember that time you drove us out to that place off Coronado?"

"Yeah, okay. Enough with the good-time gang. What's our next step?" Brady stood to stretch his legs.

"Hey, is that you?" Archer asked.

Brady spun toward the east. "I guess so. Where are you?"

"You guys don't know exactly where each other are?"

Archer said, "I know where he's at. I can see him from my

villa's balcony."

"I was on my way to locate him when I took your call."

"Come on, guys, y'all have got…"

Brady didn't hear the report of the gunshot until after the bullet struck. He tumbled on to his back across a gutter on the building's edge.

"Shot fired," Archer called out.

"Fuck. Brady, you okay?" Declan yelled.

Brady had taken metal to the face after the bullet struck the service shed. He wasn't unconscious, but he would have to fight from fading to black. He heard their voices coming from his cell phone, but he'd dropped it on the roof.

"I don't see him," Archer said. "Audrey, come in hot. We've got a sniper."

"He's down?" she asked.

"Don't know. He's unresponsive."

Brady fought to reach the phone. He had to warn Elena. The instant he moved, he felt the feeble gutter start to give way.

"Brady!" Willa screamed from her console in Surrender.

"You see anything?" Archer radioed to Audrey.

"Nothing."

"Willa, call Elena, and tell her I'm coming," Archer said.

"Yes, sir," she replied with a bit more composure.

Brady was listening to all of their communications, but when he tried to call out from about ten feet away, he couldn't speak. Slowly, he swiped fingers across his neck. Bloodied.

Another shot ricocheted in the small town. Brady flinched. It almost caused him to break the welds on the piss-poor construction.

"Shoot him," Archer ordered.

"I need you to counter spot for me." Audrey's tone remained cool.

"Okay. Let's take him out quick."

Willa returned to the call. "I've warned Elena. She said she's going up top to help Brady."

"No fucking way," Declan demanded.

"This is Elena. I'm patched into the line. Sorry, Declan, I get to make the calls on my home turf. Brady needs me."

Brady heard Elena's broadcast and peeled his eyes toward the left, where the rickety ladder was attached.

"I need to draw his fire," Audrey radioed.

"I see a reflection at five o'clock, due southeast. No confirmation," Archer called out.

Brady's eyes burned from the blood and shrapnel debris. He craned his neck to see Elena shimmy up the ladder. He tried to wave her down, but each time he nudged a finger or foot, the gutter separated a bit farther. He knew the fall probably wouldn't kill him, but it sure would screw him up.

"Down," he whispered.

Elena's face was mired in horror.

"Elena, get down," Archer yelled.

"I've got to save him," she replied.

Audrey snarled toward the target, "Come on, you fucker."

"Please, Elena. Get down," Declan demanded.

The third shot exploded from the sniper's concealed nest. Elena went down.

A fourth suppressed shot rang out.

"Got your ass," Audrey said.

"Great shooting, baby. I love you," Archer radioed. "I'm going their way."

"I got you covered," she said.

Declan's voice was at an uncharacteristic fever pitch. "Elena, answer."

"I'm here. I'm okay. Just a scratch. I had to get the sniper to shoot again so we could take him out, right?"

"Right. Great job, sister," Audrey said.

"Where's Brady?" Declan asked.

"I've got him back on the roof. Shrapnel to the throat. Swollen vocals for a bit, but he'll recover his signing voice," Elena joked.

Brady grunted. Then he grimaced. "Did good," he strained through a low whisper.

Elena brushed his brow and cleared the sharp shards of fragment from his face.

"Brady, I'm not going to live afraid anymore. I love you."

Declan's voice broke over the radio. "Wow, that's brave."

Chapter Thirteen

"It's done."

Elena locked her cell phone after receiving confirmation that negotiations would continue.

Brady held her. She knew he understood her worries about an actual face-to-face meeting with one of the cartel's inner circle. They were known as the Vipers. They were a dangerous group of select men who had banded together in the early years against the Mexican government and rival drug gangs.

By sundown, Elena would sit alone with Toro to discuss the exchange of data for her niece. The cartel said they were sending Toro for three reasons. He was a computer technology wizard, he was one of the few who hadn't raped Marguerite yet, and finally, he wouldn't hesitate to murder Elena if she tried to deceive him.

Archer and Audrey had returned to meet them in their third floor room after having swept the small town for any other hide spots or sniper nests. They'd actually found an ice maker and wrapped a bundle of cubes in an old shirt for Brady. He pressed it against his throat and grinned.

"Do you think they know where we are?" Elena asked.

"I don't think so," Archer answered.

Audrey furrowed her brow in what appeared to be

disagreement.

"Let me explain, honey. The cartel put the word out on Elena coming into the country. Elena, my dear, you are a very beautiful woman, but you look exactly like a Mexican woman. Brady, on the other hand, might've fit in back at the resort, but out here, he screams American. Every peasant with a rifle or a rock is aiming for him to get to you. There's a bounty on your head. Brady can be killed for free." Archer winked at Brady.

"That's what the old man said too," Brady mumbled.

"These people have no direct communications with the cartel. If someone were to bag you, they'd load you up in their wagon and wheel you to the temple's door to claim their thousand bucks."

"Until then, it's just random, uncoordinated efforts," Audrey said.

"You got it."

Archer kissed her.

"I think what's important is that they suspect or know you're with old *gringo* over there, but they don't know you're also with this badass couple of super spies too. We'll use that to help cover you for this meeting."

"So you don't think word from earlier will get back to the cartel?"

"Elena, do you really think they give a rat's ass about some punk with a gun getting his head blown off?"

"Well, yeah. Kind of."

"You may be right. In that case, we'll watch you extra close."

Audrey laid a paper out across an old, pitted tabletop. She'd sketched out the town and had already marked observation and escape points. She might have been more emotionally volatile than Archer, but the Mossad had schooled her well. Her training would soon be put to the test.

"Elena, you will meet Toro right here. We need you to arrive about fifteen minutes late."

"Why? They said specifically not to be late."

"Exactly. They want to kidnap you."

"What?" Water spit from Elena's mouth.

"Everything is most vulnerable during transition. This means you are most at risk while the day turns to night. Why do you think they said to meet at precisely eighteen fifty-five hours?"

"If I could focus enough to know when exactly eighteen fifty-five hours was, then I'd have a better idea why," Elena snapped.

Her nervousness began to creep back. It was understandable—these were the same brutes who'd raped her years back.

"Five minutes before seven, and ten minutes before it gets dark. We want you to arrive about ten minutes after that. It'll give us a chance to scout out their counter-surveillance and also allow us to use the NVGs to gain a better eye."

"Okay, I understand better, and sorry."

"Sorry?"

"For jumping at you. I'm getting the shakes about this."

Brady sat up and took her hand.

"No need for sorry. We will protect you, Elena. You've been very brave through this. Let's keep everyone safe."

"Okay." Archer leaned forward. "We can see where Audrey has positioned us to watch over you. The key points are that I'm designated to rescue you if anything goes sideways. While I'm busy being the hero, Brady and Audrey will lay down cover fire to distract and hopefully stop them."

"Not stop them—kill them," Audrey snarled.

"Elena, you cannot hesitate or resist me in any way. You must run as fast as you can, but do not try to go on your own. If you do, I will knock you unconscious and carry you out. Understood?"

She frowned but agreed.

Audrey jabbed her finger on the number six. "This is our exfil point. I've already parked one golf cart at this location. We will all jump in and haul ass out. I've positioned the other cart as a decoy on the opposite side of the town. Keys are in it and set to explode. Please, do not make a mistake and run to that cart."

"I won't resist you, Archer, but if I do, just don't hit me in the face. Do a neck chop or something from the movies."

"Deal."

"This is where I come in," Elena reported, switching to the work mode she felt comfortable in. "I've prepared this flash drive as a sample. I assumed they would've wanted to test it. They test everything. The data stored on here is legitimate but basically benign. Once they see that what I have is actual data, I'm sure we'll negotiate for Marguerite's release."

"Proof of life," Brady said.

"Yes," Audrey agreed. "Demand proof of life before you give him the sample file. And then, what's the plan for exchange of assets and verification of her release?"

"What?" Elena asked.

"If you give him the main data drive, they will just take it and kill you and her. What were your plans for making sure she was free and safe before handing over the flash drive?" Archer asked.

Elena focused on the table, unable to meet their eyes, "I have no plans."

"Maybe that's a good thing," Audrey interjected. "Let's do this. When you meet Toro, you shall demand proof of life. If he refuses, then you leave."

"Leave?"

"Yep, just get on that high horse of yours and ride off," Audrey teased. "We will be waiting and make sure no one follows you. They will reach out again. The cartel will not allow Toro to return to camp without that data."

"What then?"

"You do not give them anything but attitude until they allow you to speak with Marguerite. Once they concede, then you'll give them the sample. Allow them to play with it and gain confidence that they've got the real thing. Then tell them you will meet again in the morning. Say about zero eight hundred hours."

"What? Why not finish the deal right then and there?"

"They will grab you up once they see that the sample data is real. And yes, they will probably check inside your..."

"Don't say it," Elena gasped.

"Okay, but please be ready for this. Once they're done and you're royally pissed off, you tell them to put your niece on a plane to the United States tonight. Give them these coordinates and this phone for her to call you after they land."

"Will they do that?"

"Isn't it worth a shot?"

"Yeah, because I'm going to be so freaking angry after that bullshit that they'd better do what I say or else I'll feed that flash drive to an iguana until he shits out Cobalt code."

"That's my girl," Brady cheered.

"You have got to keep that attitude. I know you're going to be scared and maybe even want to do things to be friendly in hopes that Toro will help you or play by some contrived set of rules. Trust me, he will kill you," Audrey said.

Elena blinked back tears in the adrenaline-filled moment. She clasped her hands until her fingers tinted purple.

"I will. I promise."

"Best case is they allow you to leave after that. If so, we've secured a safe spot to bunk down for the night so we can all get some rest," Audrey said.

"What's the worst case?"

"Archer has to knock you out."

* * * *

"I need you on and focused."

"Roger that, Brady."

"What happened to Lieutenant Hottie?"

"That was the scared-of-you Willa. I'm the let's-kick-ass Willa now."

Audrey broke mic. "How about you just be the stay-awake Willa?"

"Yes, Aunt Audrey."

Elena's feet felt bolted to the floor. It was about nineteen fifteen hours and her cell phone hadn't stopped buzzing. She pulled it out from an external battery pack where it was recharging. The cartel was relentless in their effort.

Where the fuck are you

Driving to that stupid town. Got lost

You have 5 minutes or else

I am lost. Not my fault

Elena tried her best to be brave. It was always easy when it was just a text message, but she knew that just outside of her third story rat-hole hotel room, there waited a man called Toro. Translated as "bull" in Spanish, Toro was notorious. He was also an enigma within the cartel because, while he looked like the typical techno-computer geek, he was a seething, ruthless murderer.

"Radio check," Willa called out.

"I'm on," Brady called.

"Hear you loud and sweet, baby."

"Thanks, Uncle Archer," Willa giggled.

"Your aunt hears you too."

"Hi, team. I'm monitoring, just silently."

"Oh, umm...hello, Mr. Declan," Willa stuttered.

"He doesn't bite, Willa." Elena laughed. "Much."

The kidding around was a great stress relief. It helped Elena forget, if but for a moment, what was about to go down. She wasn't as concerned about the back and forth bartering with Toro as she was the reality that at some point, he was going to physically accost her for the main flash drive. The thought of his hands on her made her skin crawl.

Tucked away in the northwest corner of her room, she held the loaded pistol in her right palm. Each bump or the scrape of something crawling along the floor or across a wall made her breath hitch, but she kept her eyes and her focus on the door. Brady, Archer, and Audrey were already in the town's square, so she was under orders to shoot anyone who came through the door.

Her orders were simple. Stay put until directed down. There would be risk once she left the room. The other three had to maintain their positions in a triangular formation to ensure she would be safe during the meeting. That meant Elena had to exit her room and traverse three floors alone—in the dark.

Audrey had created a diversion to coincide with Elena's movement. She'd rigged the decoy golf cart parked across town so that Archer could activate its headlamps. The ploy was to make Toro think she'd just driven in, and that they'd now know where she had parked. Of course, the decoy cart was across town from where the actual extraction vehicle was staged.

"Anytime you're ready," Archer radioed. "We've got you covered."

"Thanks. Just one second."

"You can do this," came across Brady's radio. His voice was very strained but had improved.

Elena grinned at his effort. She glared through her room's window one last time. She clearly saw the cantina located directly in the center of the town's square. The tables had been cleared of the few locals. Only one man was there, and although she didn't personally know Toro, she had to assume it was him. His laptop computer was already set on the small round tabletop. The device set on the ground by his right foot looked like a remote wireless Internet router, or a hotspot, as she liked to call it.

He wasn't big or an imposing man from where she looked, but what was unmistakable was the rifle he had laid next to the laptop computer and his sinister reputation. Dressed in a starched white cotton button-down shirt and khaki pants, his wiry frame looked comfortable in the July heat of the early evening.

Elena stuffed the dummy flash drive in her bra and debated whether to carry the pistol or not. She figured it best to leave the weapon out of the equation. If one of her three cover team members couldn't shoot him, she'd be of no use. She padded around in a small circle and also debated using the bathroom, but between the toilet filled with old refuse and new creepy crawlies, she figured she'd just hold it.

"I'm ready to go," she said.

"You got the flash drive?" Audrey asked.

"Check."

"You got the cell phone for Marguerite?"

Elena's fingers flashed across the table's top until she found the cell phone Audrey had given her earlier.

"Check."

"You feel like being a hard nose negotiator no matter what that prick Toro says?"

"Check."

"Good, then let me count down from sixty before you actually walk out to meet Toro. I need to fire up the decoy golf cart."

"Check. On your count."

"Team, I know I said I was riding this one on mute, but just to let you know that Cade has rerouted and is arriving in Guatemala any time now. He'll connect with Darcy, Brant, Max, and Jade. They'll all rally just across the border from Campeche."

"Great news. Thanks, Dec," Archer whispered.

"Shane and I will touch down within the half hour to round out the team."

"I thought Cade got shut down at the customs crossing. How did he get across Mexico and into Guatemala?" Audrey asked.

"Officially he's not in Guatemala. He's actually back in Dallas, but his parachute and possibly a human life form strapped to said parachute jumped from an escort flight without authorization."

"No shit. Go, Cade," said Brady.

"You know he's got a debt to pay," Declan said. "Get this done."

"Roger that."

"On my mark. Sixty, fifty-nine, fifty-eight…"

Elena tried to turn to walk out of the room, but her feet wouldn't move. She was scared stiff. She struggled—nothing. She considered yanking each leg with her hands until they bent. Finally, she looked up and asked God to give her the courage to do this. She needed to honor her father, whom the cartel murdered. She needed to save her niece, whom the cartel would try to break, and she needed to reclaim herself for the life she now wanted to live and share with Brady Scott.

"You can do this," she mouthed and then she smiled with resolve.

"Thirty-three, thirty-two…" Audrey's countdown continued.

Her eyes grew big to capture any available light. Her ears were tuned in for sounds uncommon or sudden. She heard the rumble of the decoy golf cart in the distance and knew she had to hustle to make her mark.

"Twenty-two, twenty-one, twenty…"

Elena reached the stairs at the far end of the balcony and eased out her right foot to feel for the landing of the first step. She'd forgotten about her sprained left ankle, suffered during her fall early that morning. Her mouth drew back against her teeth because it was sure hurting. She bit back a moan and quietly gimped down the top flight of stairs. She landed safely onto the second floor landing.

So far, so good.

She slipped her hand gently over the railing and took the first step onto the rickety staircase. Her heart stuttered. There was a figure in the shadow. Big and hunched. It pressed into the corner with anticipation. She was again unable to move. It felt like the bones had melted inside of her legs.

"Sixteen, fifteen, fourteen…"

"Where are you, Elena? I should be seeing you by now," Archer asked.

"Big man in dark. Bottom of stair." Her voice quivered.

"Maintenance man," Brady said.

"You sure?"

"Think so. Saw him on the way down earlier."

"Think it's okay to go down there?" She sounded almost childish.

"Yeah, it will be fine. Now move. You broke my count. Ten, nine, eight…"

Let's do this.

Elena inhaled as her swollen ankle crunched on the ground floor landing. Her eyes felt big and wide as she eased past the lump of clothes and heavy snoring. She exhaled to clear her thoughts once past. It was time to get her attitude on.

"Four, three, two, one," Audrey counted.

Elena entered the streets void of light and emerged beneath the soft wash of a dull yellow cantina bulb.

"Hello, Toro. I'm Elena."

Chapter Fourteen

Toro stood to greet her.

He was shorter than Elena's five feet eight inches, but he carried himself much larger in standing than stature. There was no cordialness in his tone, but it seemed he wanted to appear as a refined gentleman. She knew the truth was he was nothing of the sort.

"I'd like to say my pleasure, but you've compromised your niece's safety by this unfortunate delay." His dirty fingernails lingered across the top of Elena's knuckles. A scowl slashed beneath his pencil-thin mustache.

Elena patted his shoulder.

"How about we cut the bullshit? I'm here, so if you want to deal, let's deal, but please, stop pouting like a little girl. It's unbecoming."

Elena's mind exploded after hearing those words come out of her very own mouth. She knew she had it in her, but she hadn't realized how strong she'd become through everything that led up to this.

It's game time.

Toro's black eyes peered into the distant night. She knew he had watchers, but she was confident her watchers were better than his. It was time to start talking deals. She anticipated his resistant nature, but she had hoped that once face to face, she'd convince him to play it for a straight-up exchange.

"I can assure you I'm no little girl. Do you have the disk?" He held out his open hand as if he expected her to drop the flash drive into it right then.

"Proof of life, Toro."

Toro pressed his thumb and index finger against the center of his top lip, and spread them out to run along the narrow black line of coarse hair below his pointed nose. His sneer looked as though he enjoyed the contact.

"So, you want proof of life? Show me the flash drive first."

"Listen to me, you little *puta*. I flew and then drove all the way to this fucking hellhole for my niece. Do you really think I'd come without the data?"

"I'd suggest you…"

Elena stood tall and raised a finger to quiet Toro.

"Do not insult me. I'm not the little girl your thugs raped seven years ago. I will honor my side of the agreement, but you will honor yours too."

Audrey whispered into Elena's concealed earpiece, "Whoa, sister. Calling him a bitch might be going a bit too far. More negotiating. Less agitating."

Elena nodded her head to acknowledge Audrey's instructions. She eased back into the wooden chair.

Toro craned his body over the edge of the table.

"I must say, I was not expecting you to behave in such a hostile manner. Obviously, you do not understand the process nor the respect owed our organization." His voice never rose but it slid to sinister in tone. "I was prepared to trade you one asset for another asset, but your insolence has caused me to decide otherwise."

Toro slammed his hand against the round-top table. His

laptop wobbled and the glass bottle of soda rocked back and forth before tumbling over and rolling off onto the dirt floor.

Elena's intuitive response was to recoil and apologize, but she steeled herself and refused to be victimized by the cartel ever again.

"Toro. What you do is ultimately up to you. If you want to move forward, then get my niece on the phone. If not, then I've got a long way to travel to get back home."

Toro tapped his uncut fingernail on his front tooth. His eyes shifted back and forth across the empty streets. She knew he was within the highest circle of the cartel, so he wouldn't have to consult with bosses. This was completely his decision to make or deny. His sinewy muscles twitched like guitar strings as he seemed to externalize his thought processes.

"You have the disk?"

"Yes, it's in Xpujil."

"Ah, I see."

More silence.

Elena began to move, but then she heard what sounded like Archer instruct her to just wait him out. She relaxed her arms and her body rested back into the chair.

"Voice only."

"Video. I want to see how you've treated her."

Elena wanted to see the chamber as much as she wanted to see Marguerite. She needed to gain as much intel about her niece's location as possible in case they needed to plan a rescue raid.

"That's a tough one. For my troubles, what shall I receive in return?"

"Data."

"All of it?" His lazy eyelids popped to life.

"No, naughty boy, but enough to keep you busy tonight."

Toro grinned at her reference to naughty boy. He really was delusional.

"What else do you have to keep me busy tonight?"

Archer croaked, "Ewwww."

"Radio silence," snapped Declan.

Elena wanted to laugh, but felt the same as Archer.

She feigned a sly giggle. "I'm sure the amount of data on this flash drive will be plenty for now."

"Oh, so it's here, with you?" he asked sharply.

She shoved back into her seat and realized that he wasn't a love-sick flirt. Toro processed every word of their conversation with only one goal in mind—securing their data.

"I didn't say that, Toro."

She tried to reaffirm her position, but she realized her adversarial act of defiance had been compromised because she'd fallen for his soft-sale tactic.

Damn, he's good. Just like the serpent in the garden.

His eyes bathed her from head to toe. "Where are you hiding it, then?"

"Well, it's not up my hoo-ha."

"What?"

"Nothing. It's an American expression. Let's make that call to Marguerite."

"Voice?"

"Video."

Elena fidgeted while Toro pretended to have difficulties making a connection with the cartel's base. She wanted to look around but knew that he would interpret that as her giving away the location of her backup. Eyes forward, Elena looked only at Toro.

"I seem to be out of service. Maybe we can relocate to a higher location?"

"No."

"No?"

"I thought we'd cut through the crap. Video call in exchange for the data sample."

"We did, indeed."

"Then stop thinking with your little head and get this done. I know there is cell service here. I also know you're sitting next to a wireless router and signal booster."

"You're a smart lady. I admire that."

"You must not really admire that, otherwise you'd stop trying to bullshit me and play it straight. Now, please connect us via video."

She mashed her hiking boots against the hard-packed dirt floor as the chirping sound of Toro's phone began to ring. The dull ache in her left ankle helped her remain centered. She told herself to be calm. Of course she was expected to love her niece, but an overexpression of emotion would signal weakness. It would place Toro back in charge in their role-playing charade.

The screen burst to light, and an unknown man's gnarly face was plopped right in the center of it. Toro spoke in hushed tones and secret phrases before the man disappeared from view. He was careful to prevent Elena from seeing the blank screen that only showed an empty room. Suddenly, Marguerite's face appeared as close to the screen as the man who answered the video call.

"Remember what I told you," Toro threatened Marguerite in a low murmur.

"Yes, sir," she cried.

Elena was sickened to watch the interaction.

"Here. Make it fast." He shoved the phone against Elena's chest. She fumbled it but quickly recovered and focused her attention on the screen.

"Marguerite?"

"Hello, Aunt Elena. I'm fine."

Her face had makeup that looked like a man had hurriedly smashed powder and colors against her almond-colored skin.

"I love you." Elena sniffled.

Stay strong.

"I'm fine," she repeated robotically.

"I'm coming for you, baby. Hold on."

Anger wrapped itself around Elena as she assured her beloved niece of something she wasn't sure she'd deliver—safety.

"I'm fine."

"Enough," Toro barked before he grabbed the cell and mashed the *end* button to again blacken the screen.

Elena dropped her head as if it had come unhinged. Her hands began to cross and uncross in her lap, but she knew it wasn't the time to unravel.

"Stay strong, baby," whispered Brady.

"I will, baby."

"You will what? Who is baby? Who are you talking to?" Toro demanded.

He reached out for her, but she slapped his hand away.

"I'm talking to myself, and I will save Marguerite. You can bet your bald ass on it, Toro."

She shoved her thumb and index finger beneath the neckline of her blouse and into her bra, pulling out a matte black flash drive. Squeezing her fingers around it, she closed both eyes and focused on her breathing—in and out—in and out.

"Thank you, Toro."

"For what?" His anger at again being insulted was more visible.

"For allowing me to speak with my family member."

She uncurled her fingers and let the flash drive slide from her palm and onto his laptop's keyboard.

He watched as if in disbelief that it was so easy, or as if he expected something else to follow. But no. Elena wanted to shift strategic gears and reward him for "good behavior." She hoped it would pay dividends later in the really tricky part of the process when it came time to secure Marguerite's release.

"Just like that? What's the catch?"

"There's no catch. While I understand you live in a vile world where honesty means nothing, I do not and will not live in that world. We made a deal—video call for data."

Toro held the small device between his fingers. His eyes narrowed and the furrow of his thick brow pulled his already bushy eyebrows into a single line. She almost laughed at his primitive actions. It was like he'd never seen the technology before.

Suddenly, he threw the flash drive on the ground.

"Now give me the real device," he demanded.

"Hey!" She reached for it. "That's sensitive information."

Toro kicked it into the street. His dark forearm trembled as his hand gripped the tabletop. His eyes lifted but never made contact with her. She knew he was looking for his men—or hers.

"That's crap. I want the real data. The entire scrape, not this sample of junk."

"I should've known you couldn't be trusted. I told you, I do not have the full device with me. I will not give it to you until my niece has landed safely in the United States."

"Why not just ask for a miracle, because that's what it'll take to get what you want." He howled with laughter. "Give me the disk."

Two men appeared from nowhere. They marched with stiff, scissored legs until standing at attention before Toro. He held his palm open and glared at her.

This is it. Stay strong and go for broke.

"*Yo, stupido.* What don't you understand? I don't have the full flash drive with me. I'm not crazy enough to bring it until Marguerite is released." She knew she needed a big scene. It was the only way to make him understand. To shock him into believing her. So she dug in her heels and shoved back, the old wooden chair crumbling apart behind her.

The two men, one about her height and the other one much shorter, but crazy thick with muscles, stepped back a bit. They watched her hop over a slight curb and onto the street before lunging her way.

"Don't put your hands on me," she snarled.

They stopped and she groaned as she tugged at her left boot, and then used her swollen foot to kick off her right. She dropped her khaki pants down to the ground while all three men froze in confusion. Next, she yanked the lightweight long sleeve shirt up, over her head, and threw it to the ground too. She stood there in the still of the night in nothing but a bra and panties.

"Not convinced?" she challenged them.

She stripped her bra off and then stepped out of her panties.

"Now, Toro. The choice is yours, but I'd pick up that flash drive with top-secret information and shove it into your computer or up your ass. It really doesn't matter to me, but I expect you to believe me when I tell you I don't have the full flash drive."

He averted his eyes and flipped his fingers for her to get dressed. He also directed the taller henchman to retrieve the flash drive.

"Son of a bitch," gasped Archer. "Baddest thing I've ever seen."

Elena wanted to smile as she dressed, but the overwhelming pride that rose inside was almost more than she could bear. She'd faced her demons and kicked their ass. Yes, indeed, she'd not be a victim to anyone ever again. Even if it meant taking all of her clothes off.

"You again surprise me, *Señorita* Elena."

"Toro, I'm not looking for trouble by coming here. I've got a product because you took my niece. I know how the game is played. Don't forget, you killed my father because he refused to produce a product for you. I am delivering a sample to show you good faith."

"We shall see."

Toro powered up his laptop. The screen was reflected off of the pair of thick black, horn-rimmed eyeglasses he'd pulled from his pocket. He fumbled the flash drive before finding the port to insert it.

Elena pulled up another chair and kicked the one she'd collapsed to the side. She leaned back and tried to look casual as she watched charts and graphs pop into each reflective lens. She also watched Toro's eyes rapidly scan back and forth across the eleven-inch computer screen.

He was quiet for a long time.

She began to bite at her fingernail but shoved both hands beneath her knees instead.

The slightest, most maniacal grin first appeared as a hint of satisfaction, and erupted as a fissure of excitement. It had worked—she'd deceived him.

"This looks okay."

"Okay, my ass. It's the most valuable data you've ever put your paws on."

"My dear, you've been in the United States too long. You've lost your decorum."

"You mean like kidnapping and killing?"

His head swiveled toward her. "I'd mind my tongue if I were you."

"You're not me. Now don't bullshit me, Toro. That information alone is worth millions. I don't want your money—I want my niece."

"We'll see."

"You have until tomorrow morning." Elena tossed the phone and note that Audrey had given her on the table. "I want Marguerite to call me from this cell phone once she touches down in the United States. She is to be delivered to these coordinates. There will be someone waiting for her. Just land, drop her off, and fly away. Simple."

"Do you really think it's that simple?"

"If you want the jackpot, it better stay simple."

"That's only half of the deal."

"Once she calls me, I'll message you and meet back here to deliver the entire flash drive. Then you go back to your hole in the wall and plug it in."

"How do I know you can be trusted?"

"Damn, Toro. You've seen me naked. How can I not be trusted?"

"True, but I saw you naked about seven years ago." He licked his lips.

"Stay calm, Elena," Brady radioed.

"No, you saw a child naked seven years ago. That is disgusting, and so are you."

"We'll agree to everything, except prior to dropping the girl off, I want you in my office setting up the data on our secured network. Just to be safe. You understand?"

"Then what? You kill me?"

"Ha, like you said, I've seen you nude. Why would I want to kill you?"

She eased up from the chair and pointed to the phone she'd given him.

"I'll be expecting Marguerite's call in the morning."

"Don't hold your breath, young lady."

Elena began to walk away. Before she disappeared into the void, she called back to him.

"Save your threats, Toro. Just do as I said—simple."

Chapter Fifteen

"I'd kiss you if there wasn't a hit squad of rabid mercenaries after us."

Brady appeared out of nowhere to intercept Elena. To distract the cartel after their meeting, she had been instructed by her team to head back toward the decoy golf cart. While Audrey and Archer covered their movements, Brady and Elena would circle back behind them.

The cartel hit men assigned to follow Elena would have a nice surprise waiting.

"Got her."

"Roger that," Audrey said.

Brady saw the reflection of light that came from the decoy golf cart headlight remote activation. He knew they had about a twenty-second count to clear away from that side of the town. He grabbed Elena's hand and began to run.

"Arggg." She stumbled.

"I'm so sorry. I forgot about your ankle."

Brady bent down and swooped her from the ground. He took off with her in the fireman's carry position. It looked awkward because she was draped over his shoulder with her head hanging over his ass. But it was the most efficient way for him to carry her from the area.

The booming explosion rattled the small town. Brady felt shock waves of heat ride up the back of his neck, but he kept jogging.

"You okay?"

"Yes, but I think my eyebrows were singed off." She tried to laugh but Brady heard how the jostling affected her speech.

"I think we're okay now." He set her down.

"Why did the golf cart explode?"

"Ever heard curiosity kills the cat?"

"Yes."

"They got curious. It went boom."

"Won't that mess up tomorrow?"

"No worries. They'll be very ready to deal in the morning."

"How can you be so sure?"

"I hid a camera in our room, along with clues that made it look like you were there alone. Obviously, they ransacked it. I also planted a few documents and a passcode that allows them to discover a cache of data in a security cloud. Once they crack into that cloud account, they'll find MacKenzie data. A stingy download will show them that the data matches the data you gave them on the disk."

"It's a flash drive." She rolled her eyes.

"Whatever. The thing is, they suspect what you gave them is high-level insider info. Once they feel like they've gone behind your back to confirm it, they'll have no choice but to negotiate."

Elena stopped hobbling and leaned against one of the mud and stick huts on the outskirts of town. They were still several hundred yards away from Archer and Audrey, but she seemed to be suffering from the injured ankle.

"You okay?" Brady helped stabilize her.

She pulled him in and pressed her mouth hard against his. Brady flinched for only a second, but then sank into her embrace.

His body was still on high alert, as he knew those killers who survived the blast were still looking to put a tail on Elena until the morning's meeting. But he'd long dreamed of her kiss, and killers or cartel be damned, he was going to enjoy the moment.

"Wow, what's that for?" he whispered in her ear.

"I feel alive."

"Yeah, that felt pretty alive to me, too."

"No, Brady. I was scared to death back there, but suddenly it all faded and I realized who got to make the decisions for my life—me. The victim is gone—the old and new Elena is back."

"Can I be honest? I really love the new Elena." Brady hugged her before tossing her arm over his shoulders and nudging her to move again. "But we do have to make it to the rally point soon."

"Coming?" Archer asked over the radio.

Brady heard Archer's question but before he replied, he saw shadows that danced between two dilapidated structures. He pulled back on Elena and motioned for her to squat down in the darkest area behind the burned-out building they had attempted to use for cover.

"Repeat, are you coming to our location?"

Brady recognized the tense tone in Archer's voice. Their little kiss had placed them behind the timeline for extraction. The longer they lingered, the greater their chances were of getting trapped. The figures were too close for Brady to speak without being detected. He clicked the button on his headset that caused the squelch to crackle twice.

"Roger that. You can't talk because of company." Archer interpreted the nonverbal signals.

Brady turned to Elena and pressed his finger against his lips. She nodded and knelt down. She almost disappeared into the ink black spot at the western corner of the structure.

Brady inched toward the break between the buildings. The light from the cantina in the center of town was casting the two long shadows. The same light would also limit Brady's vision because he'd have to peer into it to make out the bodies. He knew the poor locals had already been through enough, so he didn't want to over escalate the situation in the event they were just being forced to stand watch. On the other hand, if they were carrying weapons, they had to go.

He made sure not to lean against the wall. That would create sound to give away his position. Brady looked between the gap until he spotted two men standing about eight feet off the street. They looked casual enough, until he spotted the pistol in one man's hand and the machete in the other.

Damn, I hate machetes.

There was no way around the guards. They were already at the most outlying stretch of town. Neither did he want to fight them. He never doubted he'd beat them, but the attention drawn by fighting would attract others.

"Still okay?" Archer asked.

Brady clicked the squelch button.

"Roger that."

Archer didn't say it, but time was getting thin. He had to make a move. It wasn't in the Navy SEAL manual, but it had worked before. Brady picked up a medium weight rock. He heaved it as far as he could in the opposite direction—and waited. Seconds later, he heard the thud and smash against what sounded like old tin. The two men, who looked to be in their early thirties, jumped at the sound. Brady held in a chuckle. That trick worked every time.

The two men, dressed in their baggy clothes and oversized hats, shuffled out of the alley and moved clumsily toward the sound. Elena, who he assumed had seen the ruse, was already by his side and ready to make a run for it.

"Moving," Brady said over the mic.

"Roger," Archer replied.

Brady and Elena sprinted past the open gap between the two old buildings. It was no more than about fifteen yards. They'd cleared the other side, but it wasn't as pitch black. Light from other sources helped soften the effects of a moonless sky.

"Be careful where you step." Brady helped her traverse over scattered debris.

"Thanks, Brady. My ankle is killing me."

"I know, but they're just up ahead."

"Do not move, or I will kill you," slurred an ancient but excited voice in Spanish.

The man racked the slide on his shotgun. The sound was unmistakable and unnerving. A shotgun at that range would shred both of them.

Brady froze. "Okay, but don't shoot, mister." He also spoke in fluent Spanish.

"I knew where you were heading. I'm not stupid."

"No one said you were. You're much smarter than the others. You caught us."

"Do not make fun of me," the man growled.

Elena bumped her hip against Brady's. He glanced at her. Her facial expression showed that he should look at the man. But Brady shook his head no. He'd think of an escape, but not at the moment.

She tapped him again.

He ignored her.

"Not making fun, sir. You caught us fair and square."

Brady had an idea as he sensed the man had moved closer. He carefully slid his feet back so that he'd be within grabbing distance. If the man was as old as he sounded, Brady would have no problem grabbing the weapon. Brady hated to kill the man, but he'd always operated by the rule that if you wanted to die, you'd carry a gun.

"Maintenance man," Elena whispered in English.

"You sure?"

"Think so."

"It's me, my friend." Brady tried to sound friendly and familiar. "From the hotel."

The man jabbed the barrel of the shotgun into Brady's spine.

"I know who you are. I will be rich."

"You will be dead," said Archer. "Drop your weapon."

"Thank God it's you, Archer," Elena said.

Brady spun around to help Archer loosely subdue the old man. They'd be long gone soon and there was no need to hurt him.

"How's the ankle?"

"Still tender."

Archer took one of her arms across his shoulders and Brady took the other. The three began moving through empty spaces like a tank. Each realized time had in fact run out.

"Gringos. They are over here. Catch them," the old man began to yell.

They kept running but it wouldn't be long before they had more capable hunters on their ass.

"Why didn't you gag him?"

"Shit, Archer, I thought you did."

"You grab his gun?"

"No. I thought you did." Brady laughed through snorts of air.

The three of them fell to the ground as buckshot pellets from a shotgun's blast ricocheted off the building and junk cars strewn around the area. Archer rolled to his back and leveled his compact submachine gun between his knees. Brady grabbed his elbow before he opened fire.

"What the fuck, dude? These are peasants and farmers."

"Yeah, with guns that kill."

"Get ready," Brady ordered.

He raised his weapon and unleashed a burst of .223 caliber

firepower that was sure to stop peasants or professionals in their tracks.

"Move," Brady ordered, eyeing the golf cart.

Potshots and angry shouts began to clutter the once serene night. It was an odd combination of ruthless killers, sympathetic locals, and fearful resistance. In the middle of it all was one of their very own who'd come home to do the right thing. Brady felt the burden for Elena, who only wanted to do what any of these people would do—save their family.

"Get us out of here," Archer yelled.

They pushed Elena into the front seat. Both men climbed over the sides into the back. Normally they would've laid down for cover, but since the bullets kept coming toward them, they each knelt to prevent Audrey or Elena from getting hit. Of course, they weren't just kneeling bullet catchers. They unloaded hundreds of rounds back into the town. At this point, everyone in Xpujil was an enemy combatant.

* * * *

"This is the location Willa chose," Audrey said as she steered the golf cart while the men shoved it backward into a cluster of trees and brush.

"It looks secure. Water below this cliff behind us, a clearing in front of us, and the narrow access road that passes just in front of us," Brady observed as he helped Elena over to a flat spot beneath the thick foliage. "The girl done good."

"How about we get camp set up so we can get some rest? This has been one hell of a day for us." Archer carried his weapon over to his sleeping roll.

"Agreed, Archer. This was just the audition. Tomorrow is the big show." Brady also laid out an arsenal of weapons.

The overnight spot might have been geographically tactical,

but had seemed to stop the cartel when they wanted to get their hands on them. They'd take hourly turns on watch, but sleep was a commodity they'd need.

"Willa just messaged. She said Declan wants to have a quick conference call."

"Well, Declan is the boss, Brady. Who are we to say no?"

"She's right." Elena chuckled.

Brady punched in a number sequence on his secure satellite phone and set the receiver in the middle of their group. A dim green glow cast a faint hue on the rock. Soon a young but exhausted voice came through the speaker.

"Hello, everyone."

"Hi, Willa. It's Uncle Archer. Will you connect us to Declan?"

Elena's soft eyes shifted between Brady and Audrey. Her smile shone bright but also tired. She giggled.

"What?" Archer laughed at himself.

"Uncle Archer? Seriously, dude. We're fighting the arch forces of evil and you're worried about playing *Mister Rogers' Neighborhood.*"

"Well, I am her uncle."

"Okay, Mister Brady, go ahead for Declan."

Archer shot him a middle finger and mouthed silently, *Mister Brady.*

"Thanks, Willa. Hi, Declan. We're all here."

"Thanks. I know you're all whipped but this will only take a moment. First, I want to tell you, Elena, that what you did back there was nothing short of brilliant. Not a single one of us could've ever pulled that off in a million years. Of course, Cade claims he once got naked during a negotiation, but that was sex and Bourbon."

"Cade's there?" Archer asked.

"Yes. This freaking wild man jumped out of a freaking

airplane without telling the crew. He's lucky to be alive, but said he wouldn't miss this party for the world."

"We're glad he came."

"Okay, this is the game plan. For now." Declan laughed. "I've got the entire crew right here with me. We're going to stage in Guatemala until sunrise. There's no need trying to cross into Campeche to meet y'all unless you feel you need the support."

The four looked at each other.

"Declan, I think we'll be fine. We eliminated some of Toro's serious muscle tonight. He'll be short staffed but his goal is the flash drive. Since Marguerite won't physically be part of the exchange, it takes a lot of pressure off both sides. Once we get the call from her that she's safe in the US, then Elena will gladly give them the disk."

"It's a flash drive," Elena mouthed.

Brady whirled his index finger. "Flash drive."

"I hope it goes that easy. The two most likely contingency plans are that they will not release your niece or once they release her, they will kidnap you. Either way, I think this crew is better off focusing on a raid of their compound than covering a negotiation that Elena is obviously very capable of handling."

Elena leaned into Brady's chest. He sensed it—Declan's words, though carefully spoken, had shaken her confidence.

"What do you mean they will kidnap me?"

"Think about it. Once they release Marguerite, they lose their bargaining chip. What do they get in return, a disk?" Audrey asked.

"It's a flash drive," she insisted.

"Whatever," several voices said in concert.

"What happens if they get back to base and the disk is only a picture of snow, or it's a corrupted file or it's blank? They're not letting you off that easy. I'm sorry, Elena, but you'll become the collateral. And I don't see them letting you go."

She collapsed into Brady's arms.

"In the beginning, I didn't care about surviving. I only wanted to save Marguerite. But now, who would want to die at the cartel's hands? What can we do to fix this?"

"Declan, what are the chances of infiltrating that Mayan temple before they return to it with her? A rescue from the inside out?"

"Good thinking, Brady. That's exactly why I wanted Darcy to join us. She's the world's foremost authority on the Mayan culture. Of course, they didn't fortify the temples in 200 AD the way the cartel does today, but I think she's got a good idea for infiltration."

"Hi, guys. This is Jade."

"Hi, there and welcome to the party. Where's your lazy husband?" Archer kidded.

"Right here," Max replied in his typical drawl.

"Elena, couldn't you upload the data from the flash drive into a secure cloud account? Let the cartel download it remotely under your guidance, and once the data integrates into their RMS, they release you? Sort of like a foreign wire transfer of money."

"Thought of that, but I'm not giving them actual data."

"What?" Max gasped. "That's risky."

"I cannot risk the lives of brave security agents. What I've created is a program that combines the cannibal virus we secured from Tehran."

"Are you nuts?" Max whistled. "They'll kill you for that, Elena."

Brady squeezed her tighter in his arms.

"Once that flash drive is plugged into their network's port, it auto-activates by capturing their data and transferring it to a very secure server back in Surrender and to the DOJ mainframe. Simultaneously, the bug is permanently destroying each data byte inside their network. They'll be rendered helpless."

"It's suicide, girl."

"Jade, I can't help it. At the time, everything seemed like a good idea." Elena peered at Brady. "Now, not so much."

"Elena, I want you to try getting some rest tonight. I promise by morning that we'll have a plan to ensure you and Marguerite come back to Surrender safe and sound."

"Thank you, Declan. I trust you."

Chapter Sixteen

"Anyone thinking this is a bad idea?"

Declan paced the burned-out hull of what once was a thriving, legitimate manufacturing facility. The ravages of time and corruption had been too much for the property. Declan had become aware of the abandoned location a few years ago after the giant warehouse and assembly plant became the unofficial home to another of South America's notorious drug processing plants.

"I do," said Cade. "But what choice do we have?"

"Darcy, you probably know more about Guaxaca than any of us. What's it like?"

"Well, Declan, I wouldn't say that. I wasn't on the raid seven years ago that actually rescued Elena. But what I can tell you is that while they may have built walls or other structures inside the temple, there is no way the cartel has changed anything structural about it."

"So what does that mean for us?"

Darcy popped open the top on a long tube before spilling its contents onto the ground. She rolled it out flat. It was a detailed map of the Guaxaca temple as created by the Campeche's National Historic Preservation Society. The federal government's stamp of authenticity was affixed to the front and then each page in the roll up.

Declan held one end down flat. "Government issue? How'd you get this?"

"When the cartel assumed control of the property, the government figured they had no use for documents about the property. I'd helped develop the mapping and excavation processes, so they offered me first dibs. This document is actually quite valuable. Other than the ones scanned back at my office, this is it."

Max reached out. "The original?"

"Are you nuts?" Darcy laughed. "But as good as it gets."

"So what's their weakness?" Declan peered over the papers.

"Not much. Except two things."

"Yeah?"

"Water and waste."

"Okay, I can see that. Go on." Declan shot a thumbs'-up.

"Many people died of dysentery back then, and even still today, thanks to water and waste. Unfortunately, in third world countries and poverty stricken regions, the two things are interchangeable. Trust me—they're not."

"It's disgusting, but true. I still treat little kids while I'm volunteering with Doctors Without Borders," Lacey added.

"How does this help us?" Cade, who was half asleep and nursing a swollen knee suffered from his skydiving adventure, asked from across the room.

"Even as far back as before Christ, this advanced civilization knew to separate the two. The easiest way to accomplish that, and to provide for a free flow of air to circulate inside the temple, was to create duct trenches."

"No, Max. Not d-u-c-k-s. Ducts, like your air conditioning unit," Brant said.

Darcy's husband, Brant, who was Brady's brother, had often accompanied his wife to ancient sites under the guise of wanting to learn about the regions. Truth was, he didn't trust most foreign locations and mostly, he missed being with his wife.

Max chuckled. "I guess it took becoming a Navy SEAL to figure that out, right, Brant?"

"Hey, leave my hubs out of this," Darcy kidded.

Declan remained quiet, but he noticed the closeness of the group. They'd had their up and down times, but it was good to see that when the chips were down, they clung together—family. It had been tough since his mother, Mary, was murdered. Even the retaliation against her attackers had failed to ease the pain of loss. He also knew that Elena's father had been murdered by this very same cartel who was now threatening her niece. Declan couldn't bring the dead back from the grave, but he sure could help send those who killed there much earlier than they expected.

"All right, team. Let's start getting a plan laid out. Morning's light comes hot and early. We've got to be ready to move."

"I'm not sure the cartel even realizes how much they have going on at the site, but these points are the most obscure and remote to their main areas of operation." She pointed out red markings on the map.

Darcy continued, "As you can see, the clearings around Guaxaca remain today as they did thousands of years ago. They were strategically cleared out zones then and now. But the good news is, these locations have been allowed to overgrow, thanks to shoddy landscaping and the underground tunneling that remains. We conducted sonar echograms during our study of the area years ago for the government and discovered these series of accesses that lead into a thicket not far from the Guatemalan border."

"Why would you suspect the cartel hasn't discovered them?"

"I'm not certain they haven't, but I'd be surprised if any of them was skilled in the science of cartography or the interpretation of archeological markings and designations. But, I could be wrong." She snickered.

"Are they big enough for us to access?" Declan had his doubts.

"It depends. There's not much upright walking through these. Remember, the Mayans were not very tall to begin with. But, yes, they can be navigated."

"How long are we talking about? A couple of feet, maybe twenty yards, tops?" Max leaned close to the schematic.

"Sorry, Max. More like a mile at shortest."

"Damn. I knew there was a catch. Jade, looks like you're going in first."

His wife, Jade, rolled her eyes.

"Seriously, other than ramming through the front door, this is the best way in. Especially if you're wanting to go in unnoticed and wait for Elena to arrive in captivity."

"Shane, you're mighty quiet. What are your thoughts?"

"This is how I see it, and some of you may disagree." Shane, who looked to still be suffering from the exhaustion of the across-the-globe flight, sat up and brushed the map aside. "We have two objectives—one is to grab and erase their network data, and two is to rescue Elena. The problem is, in order for us to grab the data, Elena has to be kidnapped and made to input the flash drive into the terminal port. To save Elena once that happens, we'd almost have to be sitting at the terminal with her. I see this as a big possibility of things going to shit for her and us."

Shane peered at the others while he waited for a rebuttal.

The room was silent.

"Then what do you suggest?" Brant asked.

"Honestly? If Toro refuses to put the niece up in the air, then we let the kid stay in the castle and kill Toro and everyone with him. Next, we drive their vehicles back to Guaxaca with Audrey, or someone pretending to be Elena, in the convey. We pull the old Trojan Horse to rescue the girl."

"That's too damn risky, Shane. We're talking about an

innocent young girl," Jade said emphatically.

Her black eyes peered at Shane. Sweat glistened over her caramel complexion and Declan noticed that the emotion in her response and the tension in her frame implied that there was much more to her objection than an alternative suggestion.

"Jade, is there something else going on here?" Declan asked quietly.

"It's just… It's, you know, those girls." Her eyes filled with wetness and she turned away from the table.

She dropped her face into her open palms. Max leaned toward her, but Cade wrapped his arms around her. Max moved close to whisper he loved her.

"It's okay, Jade. That wasn't your fault back then, and neither is this. No matter what happens, we will do our best to protect everyone." Cade continued to comfort her.

Declan knew everyone in that room carried emotional scars. Max, Jade, and Cade's role in a human trafficking investigation had led to the tragic deaths of twelve young girls, who had suffocated inside a collapsed tunnel below the US and Mexican border.

Declan checked his watch. Sunrise about three hours away. Everything would change at that point.

"I'm looking for suggestions. This isn't going to be easy, but there has to be a lesser of two evils scenario. I'm tending to lean toward Shane's proposal. Any objections to fleshing it out and seeing what it might look like in reality?"

No one objected.

The group of usually super-alpha heroes was peculiarly docile. Declan couldn't put his finger on it, but he had the suspicion that it was the first time they'd all come together since his mother's funeral.

The discussions and debates continued over the next three hours. By the first ray of light to breach the rusted, deconstructed ceiling, the team had come to an uneasy consensus. Everyone understood that there were so many contingencies when it all hinged on someone else's decision. And it never helped when that someone was an irrational, psychopathic murderer like Toro.

* * * *

It was zero six thirty hours when Willa connected Declan's base camp to Brady's location via satellite phones. It was obvious no one at either location had slept a wink.

"You ready to rock this?" Declan asked.

"Yeah, sure. What time is it?" Brady asked.

"It's time to get moving, my man. We're sitting ducks in this jungle. I'm sure you're no safer."

Brady sat up. His eyes opened and he scanned the area. Something was wrong. Elena had begun to stir, Archer was still out cold, but no Audrey.

"Dec, Audrey's gone. Let me wake Archer and call you back."

Archer jolted up at the sound of Brady talking and passed his arms across the bedroll where Audrey should've been. He too sprang up in a state of panic.

"What the fuck, Brady?"

"Not sure. Maybe she went to hit the head." Brady shook Elena's right foot. "Hey, Elena. Get up, we've got a situation."

"What? Hey, where's Audrey?"

"Don't know. Archer, do you recall her getting up in the night?"

"Yeah, this was her one-hour rotation to sit watch, but she shouldn't have moved beyond the perimeter we established."

Archer rolled to his knees and went to stand up.

"No. Stay down. We might be watched for movement."

Elena's eyes were big and afraid. "Guys, this is scaring me. Tell me what's going on."

"Just stay calm." Brady slid a pistol over to her. "It might get crowded real quick, so watch your shots."

Archer craned his neck to look Brady in the eyes. Brady shrugged.

"Why wait until we're awake?" Her voice trembled.

"Mind games—intimidation."

"It's working. Please, let's find her and go."

Archer motioned for her to hush.

Brady strained his hearing in hopes of capturing a sound or a hint about what or when it was about to happen. It was silent— too silent. Whoever had nabbed Audrey damned sure wasn't a local farmer. Brady pointed to his own eyes with two fingers and then toward Archer. His fingers swept the ground around where Audrey had been sitting watch.

Archer crouched down close to the ground. He lightly swept his palm across the moist earth. Carefully, he retrieved something with his thumb and index finger. He shook his head and held it up. *Damn it.* It was the guided end of a blowgun's dart. Just as he suspected, it was a professional. They were next.

Brady tapped the earpiece. Willa's tired, weakened voice greeted him again.

"Get Declan," he said.

"He's already on. Go."

"Big change of plans." Brady gritted out "They took Audrey in the night."

"Fuck," Declan said. "That means y'all are next.".

"I know. Get the girl. It's the least we can do for Elena." Brady's words came through his teeth that were clenched together so tight, he thought they might snap.

"Damn, Brady," Declan said. "I'm sorry I wasn't there for you. This fucking cartel has caused more hell for our family than imaginable. I promise, I'll get Marguerite, and while I'm at it, I'll kill every last one of them for you."

"Is this really happening?" Willa asked through tears.

"Let me hang up now," Brady said, not wanting to disconnect. "What's the plan?" he asked Declan.

"Keep your eyes open and kill as many as you can."

A loud crack had Brady's neck twisting to the east. His brow furrowed. He glanced over at Archer. They both brought their weapons up to a ready position. *Crack.* Then there was a scream. Brady snugged his finger against the trigger. The three of them formed a triangle to cover as many different positions as possible. He knew that Archer was also aware that it was really about protecting Elena. They'd be overrun, but the objective would be to terrorize her into surrendering the data.

Brady picked up on the sound again. It wasn't so distant, but it was closing fast. He glanced over to Archer, who shrugged. Swarms often sounded just like that—a swarm. But this attack sounded unconventional. Either way, they were going to unload and reload as often as they could, until they couldn't.

"Ready yourselves," Archer said as the crashes began to close in.

"Aim high," Brady offered as he now heard hard breaths on the other side of the golf cart that moved toward them without stopping.

"They're here," Archer called out.

Elena collapsed between the two, as Brady and Archer lifted their barrels.

Brady sucked in a deep breath. It might be the last breath he took. His eyes swept up at the thud against the golf cart, and out of nowhere and through the morning's hot, muggy air flew Audrey.

She was completely nude, and her body was covered in blood. She hit the ground, and Brady saw the knives she held in each hand. It was surreal.

"Follow me. Now," she hissed like a serpent.

Brady wobbled to get up. He was so shocked and relieved by the sight that his mind and body weren't communicating. Archer pulled at him. He pulled at Elena. Audrey never slowed down as she ran headlong off the cliff. Archer followed his wife without hesitation.

"I can't." Elena froze.

"You will." Brady pulled her over with him.

Chapter Seventeen

The river's raging waters eventually gave way to a much calmer flow. Brady pulled Elena out of the slight current and guided her toward the sandy river rock bed along a muddy beach. She coughed and spewed water. Brady kept watch while she recovered.

Both had scrapes and skin discolorations that would soon turn to deep purple and yellow bruising. Brady had a nasty gash above his left eye. It looked like he'd hit himself with his weapon when he jumped or landed.

"I need you to move into cover," he told her.

"Why? Are we still in danger?"

Surprisingly, Brady's compact submachine gun was still strapped around his neck. Elena marveled at that and tried to regain her composure. "I don't want you to leave me."

"I've got to find Archer and Audrey. They should've surfaced up here. After hitting the water, I lost track of them."

"I'm coming." She clung to his wrist. All he had left on were his khaki shorts.

Brady knelt in the shallow water. "I've got to swim back upstream. You'll never make it with your injuries. You'll be fine here. Give me fifteen minutes. I'll be back—I swear."

Reluctantly, she agreed. Brady helped conceal her in a cove

less than twenty feet from the water's edge, his knife hidden in her pants pocket, just in case.

"I can't do this anymore," she said, putting her hand on his arm.

He jerked against her hold, and then his face went blank.

"What are you talking about?" he asked.

"I can't not tell you how I feel."

He started breathing again and a smile etched his face. "And how do you feel?" he asked.

"I love you," she told him sincerely, and then she moved into him so their bodies touched. "And I want to kiss you."

His smile was full now, with a wink of dimples in his cheeks, and he said, "Don't let me stop you."

Her lips found his easily and she put everything she had into the kiss. Every bit of longing, every need, and every hope. She wanted to give him all of her.

When they pulled apart, they were both panting, and she could feel his desire for her. It didn't scare her. It excited her, and she suddenly found herself ravenous for him.

"Feel free to tell me you love me any time you'd like. I'll never get tired of hearing it. And I really want to be naked with you."

"Thank God," she said on a laugh.

He kissed her again and said good-bye, and then he slipped quietly through the wooded area and vanished into the river's cold waters. Elena backed deeper against the hollowed-out tree. Her eyelids weighed heavier and heavier with each blink. She dozed off and dreamed of a white knight who'd come to save her.

Things were just starting to get good when his hand caressed her cheek and his lips touched hers. She sighed as he deepened the kiss.

"Wake up, sleeping beauty," he whispered.

She jerked against him. That wasn't Brady's voice.

It was Toro.

"How the hell did you find me here?" She shuffled her heels into the slippery moss-covered ground and moved out of his reach.

"I want my disk. You promised me. Remember?"

"Yes, but we were going to call to set up where to meet. You tried to overrun us back at the camp, so now the flash drive is lost. You should've waited."

"Waited?" he asked. The calmness in his voice terrified her.

"Who's trying to kill me?" she asked.

"Everyone," he said, shrugging.

"Why?"

"You have a high bounty on your head. Everyone from militias to farmers are hunting you. I hear there's a lethal force of mercenaries in the area looking to collect on the bounty. You better be glad I found you first."

"The data," she panted. "It's back at the camp. You should've waited, Toro. I knew you couldn't be trusted."

Toro's expression waxed flat and cold. He bent over and grabbed a handful of Elena's wet hair. He jerked her up and off her ass. She crumpled under the weight on her left ankle.

"I'm not a child to be given instructions."

Toro jerked her hair harder, but she wouldn't scream. She gripped his fist but he shook her head violently. His smashed his right palm into the left side of her face. The sound resonated inside her ear and made her dizzy from the concussion. She fell to all fours.

"Yes, like a dog on your knees. This is the way you were when I raped you years ago. You liked it. I know you did. Right?"

Water poured from her eyes. Her vision blurred between the drops. "Monster," she screamed.

"You think so?" he asked, his voice saccharine sweet. "Thank you for the compliment."

His boot sank into her side, and she cried out as the pain registered in her brain. The wind was knocked out of her, and she felt the crisp crack of a rib. She rolled onto her other side and wheezed as she struggled to catch a gasp of air.

"You always were disrespectful," he said. "Ungrateful, *puta*. I came all the way here to talk to you about our trade and this is how you behave?"

"Where's Brady?"

He bellowed, "Why would I give a shit? Why don't we worry about the information you stole from me? Where is it?"

Toro drew his right foot back again.

Elena flinched. "Please, no. No more."

"Give me the disk."

"It's at the camp. I told you," she pleaded.

Thwack

He slammed his foot into her shoulder and neck. It glanced into her jaw and snapped her teeth shut. Elena moaned, not sure her teeth hadn't cracked.

"I'm not going to keep asking you. There's nothing at the camp. If I had to bet, I'd say it's inside of you." He sneered.

Even in her agony, his tone sickened her.

Already in a fetal position, she tried to block her face. His fists rained down over her head and back, but she stayed tucked tight.

"I've been in you many times before, so this one won't be much different." He panted, out of breath from the swings he had thrown.

Toro viciously tugged at her clothes. Elena begged, but couldn't form the words to plead. She tasted the coppery tang of blood in her mouth. Her tongue darted over her teeth and lips but stopped at the unnatural feel of broken, torn flesh.

Elena resisted the best she could. She understood that once he had the flash drive, he no longer needed her or Marguerite.

This was a fight for both of their lives.

In the flurry of punches and pulls, she suddenly felt the slimy cold of the ground on her bare back. Toro towered over her with the shredded shirt in his fists. He patted each pocket and hem to check for the device. Elena ran her hand down the side of her torn pant leg. Relief coursing through her at what she found.

"You bitch. Where's that disk?" He dropped down with fists balled to strike.

Elena rolled from her right shoulder and onto her back. She then drove the razor-sharp tip of her KA-BAR knife into the soft space above Toro's chest and below his chin. His already downward punching momentum and her desperate upward lunge caused the blade of the knife to easily enter and then efficiently slide through his throat until it felt like the tip had exited the back of his neck.

Toro clasped his throat. He danced around on the slippery shore before flailing backward into the brush. The earth was quickly painted a bubbly crimson before fading into a dark burgundy. Turning away, Elena scrambled on her hands and knees to find her scraps of a shirt. It didn't matter though—she draped what was left over her shoulders.

She feared he had others waiting nearby. She couldn't just sit and wait for more. Her hand was careful not to touch his body, but she jerked her knife out of his throat.

Elena thought about Brady's words before he'd left to swim against the current. She was a strong swimmer. After all, she regularly trained with the SEALs while they visited and worked at the Surrender complex. She spied up river and wondered what might've actually happened to the three of them that they never returned.

She knew Toro's body had to be hidden. She didn't want his henchmen to pursue her too quickly. His body lurched and grabbed onto the stumps and roots that led from the water's gentle wave to the jungle's unforgiving canopy as she dragged it away.

Next, she returned to the sandy-bottomed river and began to wade back in the direction she'd come. Since Brady had stuck close to the bank, she'd try the same thing.

"Elena."

She stopped before the waters rose above her chest. She spun around but saw nothing.

"Elena, it's Brady. Stop."

"Brady?"

A quick bob up and down in the now running river, and she caught a watery glimpse of Brady. He was on the bank she'd just left. It took mere seconds to return, thanks to the tide.

"Oh, Brady. Thank God for you."

He helped her to her feet on the bank. She shivered from the cold. He held her. She noticed the blood on the bottom of his boots and that he had looked into the brush.

"I had to, Brady. It was either him or..."

"No, don't say it, my love. You never have to justify yourself. You're a survivor. You did what you had to do, and you are alive because of it."

"How did you get here?" She looked around him.

"Archer and Audrey had almost scaled back to the top of the cliff by the time I swam to find them. They hoisted me up since the mercs were gone."

"Mercs?"

"Mercenaries. They were here looking to collect on your bounty. There's also a small reward for our heads, but you're worth much more." Brady smiled.

"That only seems fair. I am the one with the flash drive, after all."

Brady held her hand and began to lead her away from the water.

"Come on. We've got a Jeep back up the hill. Unless you were really wanting to swim to the cliff?"

"I'll go with you. Always."

* * * *

Archer covered his eyes as he pulled off his T-shirt for Elena. Audrey hugged her tighter than she was normally comfortable with, but she was past the point of caring. She welcomed the embrace and held on for dear life.

Audrey herself was severely wounded. The latest injuries mish-mashed with her poor body's scars earned from brutal beatings and enemy tortures while serving the Israeli state. She'd come to wear them as badges of honor. Elena hoped she'd one day be able to embrace her scars as well. If not with pride, then at least with dignity.

"We've got a long haul. How about hitting the road?" Archer suggested.

Brady helped Elena into the rear of the new Jeep. He nestled in beside her. Audrey collapsed into the front seat and drew her hat over her eyes.

"Seven hours, but I think you can make it in five if you try."

"You're on." Archer said, accepting the challenge.

"Seven hours? Guaxaca is less than a hundred miles from here. What about Marguerite?" Elena started to panic.

"Relax, we're heading back to Cancun. We've still got rooms at the resort."

Elena began to claw her way out of the Jeep over the open-top back gate.

"I'm not going anywhere without my niece. What is wrong with you, Brady Scott?"

"Relax, Elena. She'll be waiting there for you."

"What?" She erupted into tears.

Elena tried to fan the wetness from her eyes with her open fingers, but opted to hug Brady instead.

"How?"

"Well, seems some of Declan's team wanted to bust in the temple, others wanted to kill all they could, and some of the others decided to sneak in and grab her."

"Oh, baby Jesus. This is a miracle."

"Looks like you weren't the only strong woman today."

"Marguerite?"

"Yes, her too. But it was Darcy, Jade, and Lacey who found their way through the narrow tunnel matrix. The stealthy ladies slipped right in, grabbed Marguerite, and slipped right back out."

"That's incredible. What did Declan do? He's a little bit claustrophobic. How'd he handle the tunnels?"

"The way I understood it, the guys didn't even realize the women had left. They were still busy standing by the tunnel entrances and arguing over a plan to rescue Marguerite." Brady put his arm around Elena. "But you won't hear that from Declan."

They settled back in the rear seat. She laid her head against his shoulder. They'd both been injured, but the warmth they felt soothed everything for the moment. Except one thing.

"Archer, would you mind doing me a favor?"

He tapped the brakes. "Sure thing, Elena. Anything."

"Oh, please don't stop. I just wanted you to turn up that rearview mirror for a moment."

Archer winked and flipped it up.

Elena wiggled in her seat to tug her still-wet khaki pants down to her knees. And then she shot a look at Brady.

"Uhh, you can look away too," she said. "For now."

Brady smiled. "Sorry."

"Thanks," she said gratefully. This wasn't exactly how she imagined Brady seeing her naked. She looked like something the cat had dragged in. "This thing has been driving me crazy."

Audrey opened her eyes to look back. "What is it? Your ankle?"

"No. It's that damn disk."

"It's a flash drive," the three yelled and broke into laughter.

Brady kissed her. "We'll call it anything you want."

Audrey held up the ringing satellite phone. "Looks like Willa's calling for Uncle Archer or Lieutenant Hottie. Who wants to answer it?"

"Lieutenant Hottie is occupied at the moment," Elena said, leaning in for another kiss. "And he's all mine."

From the Journal of Declan MacKenzie

March 22, 2037

Never would I have imagined I'd watch my legacy unfold. I spent my life moving from mission to mission, loving the rush of adrenaline and knowing that I had to be better than my opponent if I wanted to come back home. That was the life I loved. And it's how I thought I'd die. Especially after I thought I'd lost Sophia forever. I was hell-bent on destruction, taking chances no sane man would take. But those chances got the job done. And it built me a legendary reputation in the CIA. A reputation that allowed me to start MacKenzie Security.

But my priorities changed after I realized I hadn't lost Sophia. There was no mission more important than she was, and I knew my place was with her. Even a hardened and cynical man such as myself realized that kind of love was rare. She and I have always been stronger together than apart. MacKenzie Security gave us the kind of life anyone would consider blessed, but with that life there was always an element of danger.

There was a time, some twenty years ago, when I decided the life of danger wouldn't bring me back home to my children at night, so I promised my wife the mission where we saved Elena and her niece would be my last. And it's a promise I've kept these twenty years. I've been content to work behind the scenes and to spend time with my family. I learned after my mother's death that we only have our loved ones on this earth for a short time, and I didn't want to miss any of those days.

The MacKenzies have always put family above all else. It's how we were raised. And we're blessed that family was the legacy our ancestors passed down from generation to generation. It's a family that has withstood heartache and tragedy, but drawn closer together to heal. And though we miss our parents dearly, I know they're proud of the children, grandchildren, and great-grandchildren they've left behind.

Dane and Charlotte have done well for themselves. Dane turned his talents as a war correspondent into writing bestselling novelist. He even had a couple of his books turned into films. It was quite an experience to haul everyone to Hollywood for the premieres. Charlotte, or Charlie as the family calls her, has always been more comfortable under the hood of a car than in the limelight. Charlie's Automotive has always been successful in Surrender, but it took a lot of courage for her to make it a chain in three other cities. The gamble paid off well.

Their four children are grown and making their own waves in the world. Jayden, as a successful painter whose work hangs in museums all over the world. Rose, who fell in love at an early age with the animals on the MacKenzie ranch and decided to go into veterinary medicine. And Dempsey and Victoria, who both work for MacKenzie Security.

Thomas and Cat have beaten all odds. Who would have thought a small town doctor and one of the world's most renowned cat burglars could've had a happily ever after? Surrender eventually grew to a size where it no longer made sense for Thomas to treat patients from the office at the MacKenzie farmstead. So he built an office in town on the other side of the library. Cat says she's grateful not to have strangers roaming around her house anymore.

Speaking of Cat, she was quite an asset to MacKenzie Security for a lot of years when it came to "retrieving" certain items. I've never, to this day, seen someone with her skill at getting in and out of places without being detected. We've never been able to replace her, but she's been content with retiring from that life and raising their four children. She's turned her time as a homemaker into a popular cooking blog, sharing recipes that we're always happy to try out for her.

Three of Thomas and Cat's children are employed by MacKenzie Security in some capacity. The oldest, Griff, followed in his father's footsteps as one of two doctors in Surrender. Greta, the youngest, followed in her mother's footsteps, and I've used her for several missions that required a little more delicacy than going in with a team and guns blazing.

Riley and Maggie have always lived a life of adventure and travel, and more so than any of the others, they tend to stick to themselves and enjoy each other. It took them a while to have children, but they were blessed with three, one right after the other. And once the last one was off to college, Riley and Maggie decided to take six months for a trip around the world. They're rarely in town unless it's for a holiday, and the last I'd heard, they were on a cruise in the Mediterranean.

Cooper and Claire are usually easy to find. They're both pillars of the community in Surrender since Cooper is the longest running sheriff the state of Montana has ever had, and Claire is still the head librarian. Their oldest son, Ian, is a Navy SEAL and part of the team MacKenzie Security uses on occasion. Their other son, Colin, moved to Texas and is working with Cade out of the Dallas field office. Colin was an Army Ranger, so his skillset is very specialized and useful to the family business.

Cade and Bayleigh love living in Texas, but they make trips to

Surrender several times a year for staff meetings and family gatherings. I never would have thought Cade was capable of turning into the family man he has after the things he's lived through and done, but he proved me wrong. Bayleigh and his girls are his world, and he plays the role of overprotective father to a tee. It is a brave man indeed who approaches one of the MacKenzie girls for a date, though they can take care of themselves if truth be told. Bayleigh's lingerie shop has become one of the most exclusive and popular stores in the city, and she opened another store in Dallas so she and Cade could have lunch together most days. Of all my brothers, Cade reminds me most of my father. It's a nice feeling to have his presence in the house when we're all gathered together.

Grant and Annabeth live a quiet life. Their farmhouse always seems to be gaining a new addition or a remodel, but that's to be expected since building is in Grant's blood and he always needs a project. Annabeth has the patience of a saint.

Her boutique has done well in Surrender, but it's the little room in the back where she sells intimate items and select sexual aides that really keeps the shop well in the black. The ladies of Surrender look at Annabeth as a woman who broke the mold of having men dictate what was respectable for "their" women to buy, and she fought past town ordinances and opposition every step of the way.

The crowning moment was when she held a town hall meeting for women, encouraging them to make good use of their guest rooms until their husbands brought their thinking into the twenty-first century. MacKenzie men have always been progressive when it comes to our wives, so we were able to stand back and watch in amusement, but for a few days, there were an awful lot of unhappy men in Surrender. Needless to say, they changed their minds rather quickly and allowed Annabeth to sell her products right there on Main Street. Of course, she paved the way for other women, because a few years later when Liza Carmichael moved to town and took over her aunt's bakery, she was able to sell exotic cakes and pastries with no protests at all.

Darcy and Brant have bought a sprawling ranch that edged the MacKenzie property, and though they still live in D.C. full time, they speak often of making the transition back to Montana and retiring from city life. Brant still runs the D.C. branch of MacKenzie Security, and their son, Mac, is being groomed to take his father's position. I can't think of anyone I'd rather have at the helm. Mac is brilliant, and he was recruited by the CIA while he was still in college. He was born for the job, and he made a name for himself within the CIA ranks before I was finally able to convince him to take up the family business. He's a hell of a negotiator, and I'd be amused if I wasn't paying him so much. He reminds me a hell of a lot of myself, which Darcy tells me often made Mac's childhood very interesting.

Darcy is considered the premier expert on the Mayan civilization in the world, and she travels a lot for lectures or if new discoveries are made. But like Brant, she's anxious to leave the city life and come back to her roots. I can't imagine having Darcy underfoot again. I still remember her as a bratty kid, following us around and giving us hell at every turn. Most of my cuts and bruises as a kid were because of her. She has a hell of a right hook.

Shane and Lacey have been essential to the growth of MacKenzie Security. There was a time when I wondered if I'd lose my youngest brother. And for a while, I did. I can't imagine what it was like for him to lose his command, his leg, and his pride in one fell swoop. But I'll never be able to repay him for the sacrifice he made, because the only reason I've been able to grow old with Sophia is because of him.

Lacey has remained as chief of staff at the hospital and put us on the map as far as the latest in medical procedures and what's coming out of the R&D lab. I couldn't be prouder of the advances we've made in medicine for our soldiers, law enforcement of all agencies, and government contractors. They do the jobs no one else has the guts to and they deserve the best. I'm glad we're able to give it to them.

I've lived an incredible life, though it's far from over yet. I have no intention of stepping down from the helm anytime soon, but my focus has and always will be on Sophia and our life together. She's more beautiful now than the day I married her, and I know I'll love her more tomorrow than I do today. There's still no other woman I want to wake up next to or make love to. There's no other woman I'd rather tackle life with.

We've been blessed to have friends and agents that have become family. They've been loyal through the years and put their lives at risk countless times. Max and Jade Devlin had each moved from field ops to training new agents. Needless to say, our new agents are formidable opponents. Archer and Audrey Ryan have also moved to the intelligence side of things in the company. Audrey has skills that are irreplaceable, and Archer has contacts that are invaluable.

And then there's Brady and Elena Scott. They overcame all the obstacles and have made a beautiful life for themselves. Brady's love for being a SEAL and staying in the military outweighed every offer I made him to join MacKenzie Security over the years. I don't hold it against him. He's known now as Admiral Scott and is the chief of operations for the navy. Elena is still an invaluable part of the team, running operations from behind the console and bringing our agents home safe.

When I look back at my life, I don't think of the close calls or life-or-death situations. I don't think of the evil in this world or that every day could be the last. What I think about is growing up on this vast stretch of land with my siblings and cousins. I think about roaming free and raising hell. I think about midnight swims in the lake and Sunday dinners after church.

I think about stolen kisses in the hayloft and riding a runaway tractor through the fence while my brothers doubled over with laughter. I think about marrying Sophia in the backyard under a canopy of flowers and knowing with certainty I'd do it all over again. I think about walking with her hand in hand and watching the sunset, and I think about how our children were born in the same bed that my siblings and I were born in.

It's safe to say that the path my grandparents started for us more than a century ago has blossomed into something beautiful. Maybe someday I'll write my memoirs so the younger generations know how special their legacy is. And I think it's safe to say that MacKenzies will be around for a long time.

Discover the Liliana Hart Mackenzie Family Collection

Spies & Stilettos by Liliana Hart
Trouble Maker by Liliana Hart
Rush by Robin Covington
Never Surrender by Kaylea Cross
Avenged by Jay Crownover
Bullet Proof by Avery Flynn
Delta: Rescue by Cristin Harber
Hot Witness by Lynn Raye Harris
Deep Trouble by Kimberly Kincaid
Wicked Hot by Gennita Low
Desire & Ice by Christopher Rice

Discover the World Of 1001 Dark Nights

Collection One

Collection Two

Collection Three

Collection Four

Bundles

Discovery Authors

Blue Box Specials

Rising Storm

Liliana Hart's MacKenzie Family

About Liliana Hart

Liliana Hart is a *New York Times*, *USA Today*, and Publisher's Weekly Bestselling Author of more than 50 titles. After starting her first novel her freshman year of college, she immediately became addicted to writing and knew she'd found what she was meant to do with her life. She has no idea why she majored in music.

Since self-publishing in June of 2011, Liliana has sold more than 5 million ebooks and been translated into eight languages. She's appeared at #1 on lists all over the world and all three of her series have appeared on the *New York Times* list. Liliana is a sought after speaker and she's given keynote speeches and self-publishing workshops to standing-room-only crowds from California to New York to London.

Liliana can almost always be found at her computer writing or on the road giving workshops for SilverHart International, a company she founded with her husband, Scott Silverii, where they provide law enforcement, military, and fire resources for writers so they can write it right.

Connect with me online:
twitter.com/Liliana_Hart
facebook.com/LilianaHart
My Website: www.lilianahart.com

Discover More Liliana Hart

Dawn of Surrender
A MacKenzie Family Novella
Coming December 12, 2017

MacKenzie vs. MacKenzie...

U.S. Marshal Cole MacKenzie has been tracking the leader of the notorious Silver Creek Bandits as they leave a trail of bodies in their wake with every bank they rob. The leader is smart, cunning, and ruthless. And he's also his brother.

Elizabeth MacKenzie never dreamed her life would lead her to Montana, but she'd taken one look at Cole MacKenzie and known he was the one for her. She never imagined Cole's obsession with hunting his brother would leave her in a marriage cold and barren, wondering when he'd come home.

One heart is broken and the other is bitter, but love is a choice, and it's one Cole and Elizabeth are determined to make.

* * * *

Sweet Surrender
A Mackenzie Family Novella
By Liliana Hart

It's been twelve years since Liza Carmichael stepped foot in Surrender, but after her great aunt's death she has no choice but to return and settle her estate. Which includes the corner bakery that's been a staple in Surrender for more than fifty years.

After twenty-five years on the job, Lieutenant Grant Boone finds himself at loose ends now that he's retired. He's gotten a number of job offers—one from MacKenzie Security—but he's burned out and jaded, and the last thing he wants to do is carry the burden of another badge and weapon. He almost turns down the invitation from his good friend Cooper MacKenzie to stay as their guest for a few weeks while he's deciding what to do with the rest of his life. But he packs his bag and heads to Surrender anyway.

The only thing Boone knows is that his future plans don't include Liza Carmichael. She's bossy, temperamental, and the confections she bakes are sweet enough to tempt a saint. Thank God he's never pretended to be one. But after he gets one taste of Liza and things start heating up in the kitchen, he realizes how delicious new beginnings can be.

* * * *

Captured in Surrender
A MacKenzie Family Novella
By Liliana Hart

Bounty Hunter Naya Blade never thought she'd step foot in Surrender, Montana again. Especially since there was a warrant out for her arrest. But when her skip ends up in the normally peaceful town, she has no choice but to go after him to claim her reward. Even at the cost of running into the cop that makes her blood run hot and her sense of self-preservation run cold.

Deputy Lane Greyson wants to see Naya in handcuffs, but he'd much prefer them attached to his bed instead of in a cold jail cell. She drove him crazy once before and then drove right out of town, leaving havoc in her wake. He's determined to help her hunt down the bad guy so he can claim his own bounty—her.

* * * *

The Promise of Surrender
A MacKenzie Family Novella
By Liliana Hart

Mia Russo spent ten years working undercover, entrenched in the dregs of society before handing in her shield. Opening her own pawn shop is a piece of cake in comparison. All she needs is the bad attitude she developed on the streets and the shotgun under her counter to keep law and order. Until the day Zeke McBride walks into her shop.

Zeke knows Mia has every right not to trust him. He was the one who chose the next op instead of her. And all he can hope is that somewhere under the snarl and cynicism is a woman who can forgive. Because whether she trusts him or not, they're going to have to work together to bring down the gang that's decided Mia is their next target.

* * * *

Trouble Maker
A MacKenzie Family Novel
by Liliana Hart

Marnie Whitlock has never known what it's like to be normal. Her ability to see the future and people's innermost thoughts makes her an outcast—feared—loathed. Even by her own parents. And her father is determined to beat the curse out of her. Her only chance for survival is to escape Surrender.

Beckett Hamilton has loved Marnie since they were kids, but one horrible night destroyed any future he'd hoped for. Now Marnie was back in Surrender, and picking up where they left off is the only thing on his mind. He finds out quickly that some hearts take longer to heal, and not everyone that's broken can be fixed. But loving Marnie isn't an option—it's his destiny.

On Behalf of 1001 Dark Nights,
Liz Berry and M.J. Rose would like to thank ~

Liliana Hart
Scott Silverii
Steve Berry
Doug Scofield
Kim Guidroz
Jillian Stein
InkSlinger PR
Asha Hossain
Fedora Chen
Kasi Alexander
Pamela Jamison
Chris Graham
Jessica Johns
Dylan Stockton
and Simon Lipskar

Printed in Great Britain
by Amazon

86559407R00123